YOU'VE GOT HIM COLD

BOOKS BY THOMAS B. DEWEY

The "Mac" series:

Draw the Curtain Close
Every Bet's a Sure Thing
Prey for Me
The Mean Streets
The Brave, Bad Girls
You've Got Him Cold
The Case of the Chased and the Chaste
How Hard to Kill
A Sad Song Singing
Don't Cry for Long
Portrait of a Dead Heiress
Deadline
Death and Taxes
The King Killers
The Love-Death Thing
The Taurus Trip

The Pete Schoefield Series

And When She Stops
Go To Sleep, Jeannie
Too Hot For Hawaii
The Golden Hooligan
Go, Honeylou
The Girl With The Sweet Plump Knees
The Girl in the Punchbowl
Only on Tuesdays
Nude in Nevada

The Singer Batts Series

Hue and Cry
As Good As Dead
Mourning After
Handle with Fear

Others Novels

My Love Is Violent
Hunter at Large
Can a Mermaid Kill?
A Season of Violence

YOU'VE GOT HIM COLD

HIM COLD

THOMAS B. DEWEY

WILDSIDE PRESS

CHAPTER ONE

…like when you're closed for that day and somebody knocks on the door and when you open up you're looking at absolute doom…

This guy had trouble on him like a shroud. Fear encased him like a full-length halo. It was shiny. It scared me just to look at him.

He spoke my name with a question mark, then told me his. Charles Traven.

"You're wanted," I said. "Badly."

"Look, I have to see you—please—"

I nodded him in and showed him a chair. When I closed the door, I found myself setting the deadbolt.

"How did you know?" he asked.

"You've been on radio and television on the hour," I said. "No pictures. It was your name I remembered."

I offered him a drink and his face rejected it violently. So I waited awhile and he told me his story.

* * * *

In the early afternoon of the day before, Saturday, April 6, he had had a violent quarrel with his wife, slammed out of the house and gone on an eight-hour binge. All it accomplished for him was to make him sick in the stomach. He ran into a lot of people he had never seen before and who could not have been expected to remember him later.

At about ten-thirty, he got into a taxi and gave the driver his home address. It was a large-scale housing project with multiple entrances on four streets. He approached his apartment by way of a rear service yard and the back steps, for no reason except that he didn't feel like having to talk to anyone who might still be hanging around out front. Most of the surrounding apartments were dark. He heard quiet radio music from one, low voices from another.

He used his key on the back door and walked into a dark kitchen. The rest of the apartment was also dark and he felt relief. He had no stomach for facing his wife at this hour and, suspecting that she had gone out (probable), or gone to bed (less probable), planned to spend his night on the living-room couch.

Glancing into the front hallway, he noticed that the bedroom door stood open. As his wife invariably closed it when she went to bed, he assumed she had gone out. He was in the closet at the front of the living room, getting down a blanket, when he saw her new coat hanging in place. It having been a principal element in their quarrel, he considered it with some bitterness, then began to wonder why she hadn't worn it. This one was mink and could not have been purchased, as he estimated it, for less than seven and a half thousand dollars. He had not bought it himself.

He threw the blanket on the couch and it was at this point that he heard the tenants in the adjoining apartment get out of bed and start moving around. He didn't think about it much, just noted it. For a few minutes he sat on the couch, trying to work up enough steam to get to the bathroom and back into bed. He was a little frightened. He wasn't sure now that his wife had gone out and he couldn't face the prospect of getting the whole thing started again. He swore at her mentally for not having closed the bedroom door as usual. Then he decided that since he paid the rent and other household expenses, he had as much right to use the apartment facilities as anyone, so he got up and started down the hall to the bathroom.

At the open bedroom door he paused, planning to close it silently and lessen the chance of waking her. He leaned in carefully, reaching for the knob, and that was when he saw her. His first impression was that she was praying, but the idea was so preposterous that it lasted only while he blinked his eyes once. Then he tripped the light switch and went into the room.

What he had seen as an attitude of prayer was a parody on her actual position. From the lower waist up, she was sprawled over the bed, face down, her right knee was on the floor and her left knee raised with the foot flexed, as if she had been about to climb onto the bed after a fall, or as if she had been caught and dragged back in the process. She was wearing the same garment in which he had last seen her, a pink nylon negligee, and her hair, undone, fell about her face. One of her hands clutched a wad of the bedclothes, the other lay open. She wasn't breathing, and when he touched her shoulder he found it dead cold.

He saw that the negligee had been disarranged, pulled away from her left thigh and buttock, revealing a large and rather ugly skin blemish about which she had always been highly sensitive. A Korean veteran, Traven had seen enough death to know its face. But this crude exposure was what really convinced him. Even in coma, she would have covered that mark. This was his explanation for not calling a doctor or the police immediately. It seemed suddenly that there just wasn't any particular hurry. In passing, he rearranged the negligee to cover her. It was a small kindness, of no significance as far as anybody now knows.

He noticed a metallic glint among the loose hairs at the back of her head and saw that the thin, silver neck chain she wore constantly had been pulled around so that the clasp was somewhere toward the front of her neck. The segment now at her back was broken and the two ends slipped slowly away when he fingered them. Normally, along this part of the chain hung a small key.

He found the key in the only other place he had ever seen it, the lock of a strongbox where she kept jewelry and other things of which he knew nothing. The box was not in its accustomed place on her shelf in the bedroom closet, but sat precariously on a corner of the high chiffonier opposite the bed.

It had a fascination for him. It had stood between them, along with other items less concrete, as a symbol of mutual suspicion ever since their marriage. He had never been permitted to see or know of its contents, except for the jewelry. He remembered one day, when they were rearranging some things, he had ventured to move it out of the way. She had flown into a rage, snatched it from him and laid down the law that he was to abstain from touching it as long as they both should live. He had obeyed, largely through lack of interest, except that before her ultimatum he had actually felt no interest and after it he began to develop some. Two or three times, in her absence, he had found himself looking for the box. Each time, it had been gone. He had assumed she had hidden it or taken it with her.

When he took hold of the key, the box teetered on the high chest and nearly fell. He grabbed it with both hands, lifted it down and set it on the floor to open it. Her jewel case, a velvet-lined tray, filled less than a third of the depth of the box. Underneath was an assortment of odds and ends; a few trinkets—he remembered a brass bottle opener edged with rhinestones, a tarnished key ring on a rabbit's foot, a faded newspaper clipping featuring her as winner of a dancing contest in a Chicago ballroom. There were a pair of dice and the stub of an airline ticket to Las Vegas and return, dated some years before their marriage. Considering the size of the box and the violence of her reaction the one time he had touched it, the wistful collection of souvenirs seemed puny and inconsequential.

Not in the box, but under a pile of lingerie in a bureau drawer, he found three photographs, snapshot size; legal definition: lewd and obscene. Obviously flash shots, they had been taken in rapid succession and the model apparently had been caught unaware. The girl who had done the posing was unknown to him. He had the pictures in his hand when the knocking started at his front door.

Along in there, with a kind of unconscious deliberation, he began to build his own scaffold. Inexplicably, he put the pictures in his pocket. He replaced the jewel tray, closed the box and set it on the chiffonier with the key in the lock. The knocking grew insistent. He took firm hold of the bedroom doorknob with his bare hand, started to close it, then changed his mind and left it open. At the front door, he handled the inside knob to admit the couple who lived in the adjoining apartment. A few seconds later he handled the outside knob because the door got away from him and he tried to keep it from banging. It banged anyway and he left it ajar.

The neighbor's name was Harold Simpson. He was in his fifties, and now, in bathrobe and slippers, he was disgruntled and embarrassed. His wife, Mabel, was also in a bathrobe, but unembarrassed. She was simply hostile, as always, to him, and extremely nosy.

"What's happened here? Where's Connie?" she said.

Traven couldn't say anything. He looked helplessly at Simpson, who had a spark of human understanding and didn't like being where he was.

"Come on, Mabel," he said, "leave the guy—" But Mabel's nose was on the scent.

"I haven't heard a thing from Connie since you said those horrible things to her this afternoon."

She brushed past Traven and headed for the bedroom. Her husband stayed where he was. A moment later, Mrs. Simpson was screaming. Her husband ran into the bedroom hall. By the time Traven reached the middle of the living room, Mrs. Simpson was bearing down on him and Simpson was staring curiously over her shoulder.

"You killed her!" she yelled. "Call the police!"

Harold didn't move right away.

"Just a minute, Mabel—" But Mabel was gone, heading for their apartment. Harold compromised by going to the front door and standing there with his back to Traven.

It didn't take Traven long to reach a decision. His total condition, emotional and physical, drove him automatically away from a hopelessly overwhelming situation. He ran out the back door and kept going.

He had his car keys and he drove to the edge of his city, left the car and took a bus to Chicago. He got there at four-thirty in the morning and spent an hour in a cafeteria on the South Side, drinking coffee. He couldn't eat.

When it was light, he started walking. At eight o'clock he checked into a small hotel under a fictitious name and went to his room. He lay on the bed for a couple of hours, then couldn't stand it any longer and walked some more, winding up in a coffee shop in the vicinity of 63rd and Cottage Grove. He managed to eat a ham-and-egg sandwich and keep it down long enough to get outside. Then he lost it. This embarrassed him and he left the neighborhood.

By mid-afternoon, he was wandering around on the deserted Oak Street beach, on the North Side now. He had violent reactions of guilt and deep loss. Half a dozen times he took out the nude photos, studied them and put them back in his pocket. Early in the afternoon of this day, Sunday, April 7, he found his way to me.

CHAPTER TWO

When he finished, I wished vaguely that he would go away. But he felt better with the thing out in the open and it was my turn. Besides, there was something about him, a kind of boyish, straightforward ruggedness. He looked as if he could go a few rounds if necessary.

"Tell me," I said, "do you have any friends?"

"It was my best friend sent me to you. Pete Bowman. He's a lawyer."

I didn't know any Pete Bowman.

"He said at least you'd be able to give me advice," he said.

"Advice is pretty cheap. Didn't he have any?"

"He's not that kind of a lawyer. He's with a big firm, just getting started."

"All right. How long were you married to the woman"

"Less than two years."

"What was the fight about yesterday?"

"About the coat, mainly. Then some other—"

"What about the coat?"

"It was a mink coat! Seven, eight thousand dollars! We don't have that kind of money. So when she came in wearing it—"

"You wondered where she got it?"

"I thought maybe she charged it. She had an account—used to drive me nuts. When I saw the coat—"

"You mentioned it?"

"Yeah. She flew off the handle. Said she paid for it with her own money."

"Did she have money? An inheritance?"

"As far as I know, she never had a dime."

"So you got to yelling at each other?"

"I guess so."

"And Mrs. Simpson next door could hear it?"

"You can hear everything that goes on in those apartments."

"Did you fight that way often?"

"Yeah." He rubbed his face roughly. "It was kind of a way of life for her."

"You said something about her going out nights."

"Plenty, right from the start. We had a three-day honeymoon and then I had to go back to work. She wanted to go somewhere every night! Some bar, dancing, someplace. I couldn't afford it. In the second place, I couldn't stand the pace. I'm a draftsman in an aircraft parts plant. I have to be steady."

"Where did you meet her?"

He rubbed his face again.

"In a dance hall, kind of a taxi dance—"

"In your town?"

"There's one, the Tropical Gardens they call it." He looked at me a little sheepishly. "I know," he said. "Just out of the service, a bunch of us used to hang around there. Most of the other guys drifted away, got married. I kept going back. Connie kind of went for me—I thought. We got married."

"Did you have anything in common outside of the dance hall? Mutual friends?"

"No. I don't even know if her parents were living. They never turned up or wrote her any letters. I think she had a brother or sister somewhere, but I never met one."

He wasn't quite looking at me.

"No mutual acquaintances at all?" I prompted.

"Well—" he said reluctantly, "there was Pete."

"Pete Bowman, this lawyer?"

"Yeah. He knew her. He went with her some."

I waited, but that was all he cared to say about Pete Bowman. "When she went out alone," I said, "did she go with other men?"

"I don't know. I don't know where else she'd have got a coat like that."

"But you don't know the name or face of any man she might have been seeing?"

"To tell the truth, I kind of lost interest. Even about the coat, I didn't care, just so I wouldn't have to go in hock to pay for it."

"This was going on most of your married life?"

"Practically all of it."

"Why did you stick with her?"

He shrugged.

"You hate to give up," he said. "Anyway, she'd have stuck me for everything I had."

"Did she ever threaten to walk out on you?"

"Oh, hell, yes. I got so I wished she would."

"All right. Let me have those pictures you found."

He came up with them hesitantly.

"You say you don't know who this girl is?"

"No. I never saw her."

I laid them side by side on the desk. Traven slumped in his chair. He needed a shave and his clothes looked as if they belonged to somebody else.

He closed his eyes, squeezing them tight. I gathered up the snapshots and dropped them into my desk drawer.

"Getting around to that advice," I said, "you must realize you have only one immediate course."

His dark ringed eyes haunted me.

"Go back and turn yourself in," I said.

"But I didn't do it! Why would I come to you?"

"You've already told me that. You're a fugitive. If I advise you any other way, they'll put handcuffs on me, too. I can't help you from there."

He pushed to his feet and stood leaning slightly, like an old tree.

"What if I just walk out on you?" he asked.

"I'll have to try and stop you. If I can't, I'll have to call the police."

For a minute, I thought he was going to try to run again. But he must have been too tired, or else it had got through to him that if he would give it a chance, I might really be able to help him.

"I'm going across the street and get a paper," I said. "The bathroom's in there. Wash up and shave, you'll feel better."

He turned like a puppet and headed for the bathroom. I got my hat and went out, walked to the out-of-town-papers stand on the corner, found one from Steel City, his home town, and walked back to the office. Traven was nowhere in sight, but I could hear water running in the bathroom. I spread the Steel City paper out on the desk and read a black headline:

MAN SOUGHT IN WIFE SLAYING

There was a picture of the couple, heads together in happy newlywed fashion, that some reporter had doubtless caged out of a bureau drawer. Following the lead, a subhead drove a big spike into his coffin:

Used Abusive Language, Says Neighbor.

Mrs. Simpson got a big play. Her account was obviously one-sided and the paper made only a token attempt to qualify it. The Travens had frequent, bitter quarrels. Mrs. Traven's husband had called her vile names, threatened to strike her. It was not at all clear, the way the story was handled, how much of Mrs. Simpson's account of previous quarrels was actual overheard conversation and how much Connie had reported from her own viewpoint. On the day of the murder, Mrs. Simpson had heard their quarrel, some slamming, had heard Traven go out and after that, nothing but silence. Shortly afterward, she had gone out to the market. She was gone about an hour and on her return she knocked at the Traven door and got no reply. When she tried the door, it was locked.

I pushed the paper aside, looked at my watch and wondered what was keeping him. I looked at the paper again and it was five or six hours old. It was just possible that if there were some later developments, I could get them from a local friend without giving anything to speak of in return.

I picked up the phone, dialed, waited, talked to a few people and finally a guy said, "Homicide, Sergeant Bixler speaking."

"Lieutenant Donovan," I said.

Donovan answered all right, but to the wrong ear. I turned my head and he was standing in my doorway. He had a colleague with him, a stranger to me. There was something out-of-town about him. He was younger than Donovan, younger than I for that matter. He had the eyes and manner of a gut-shot moose.

CHAPTER THREE

Donovan's big Irish face was stiff.

"You entertaining a fellow name of Traven?" he said.

When I didn't speak right up, he took a couple of steps toward the desk. I got on my feet.

"I'll get him," I said.

The two of them were climbing my back at the bathroom door. I knocked and got no answer. The water ran loud and clear. It occurred to me he might have drowned himself.

"Traven!" I called.

Still nothing. I started to knock again and Donovan pushed me aside and threw the door open. Nobody. Brushing past me toward the kitchen, he muttered, "…pulling an old trick like that on me…"

The other one jostled me out of the way and plowed through Donovan's wake. By the time I reached the kitchen, their combined bulk was surging onto the service porch. Outside, I heard running footsteps.

From the back door of my combined office and living quarters, a narrow walk led to a wooden gate and the alley. Traven apparently had been hiding beside the steps, getting his nerve up to run.

I caught a glimpse of him through the window over the sink. He was breaking for the gate. I heard Donovan roar:

"Police! Stop!"

At the gate, Traven halted, looked back. I saw him indistinctly, his face a strange white flower on a thin, black stem. Donovan barked in a new tone.

"Hold it right there—" Then, anxiously, "Wait!"

I saw the moose-head out on the walk, his gun out and high. I ran for the service porch and the thing cracked. I was at the door in time to see Traven buckle and grab at the gate and, somewhat slowly, slide down into an awkward pile. A couple of windows went up. Donovan ran out along the walk to the gate and leaned down, doing something with his hands. When he straightened, his movements were those of an old, tired man. He came back slowly to join the other one.

"He was stopped," Donovan said.

"He was trying to get through the gate," the guy said. "You saw it—"

"He was stopped," Donovan said stubbornly.

"You going to stand here—? Look, was he with his hands in the air?"

Donovan moved away from him. I went to the sink and leaned over it and ran cold water on my head. It didn't help any. Five, six minutes passed. They came back to the kitchen. The stranger still had his gun in his hand. He waved it at me.

"You," he said, "you saw it. How did it look to you?"

I looked at Donovan.

"Who is he?"

"Sergeant Downs, Steel City," Donovan said.

I couldn't bring myself to look at him.

"What if Traven was the wrong one?" I said.

"Wrong what? He was a fugitive, wanted for murder! We had him cold."

I looked out the window.

"Well, you've got him cold now, all right," I said.

"Go on," Donovan said, "get your partner. I'll call in."

"Go by the alley," I said. "Don't bring 'em through here."

The intrepid marksman took time to glower at me while he put his gun away. Then Donovan gave him a nudge and I heard them clomping through the office. I ran the cold water, sloshing it on my face, and after a while it helped a little...

* * * *

There was a small official group around my back gate. They kept the lights and the noise low and worked with unusual dispatch.

Two figures separated from the group and came to my back door. One of them was Donovan and I opened up. Then I couldn't make myself look at the other one and walked away into the office. When I turned around, Donovan handed me a gun. Mine. Sergeant Moose-eyes was leering at me.

"What do you think now, friend?" he said. "This was in his hand."

I took it from Donovan, went to the bathroom and put the gun away.

"You always leave it hanging in the bathroom?" the Sergeant said.

"I only wear it in the shower," I said.

"What makes your friend so snotty?" he said to Donovan.

Donovan sat on the edge of the couch with his big hands between his knees. He needed a new suit. His shirt was too tight for him so that his thick neck squeezed out over the collar. I tried to figure how many more shopping days till Christmas, then remembered he had a birthday coming in July.

Sergeant Downs sat on the edge of my desk.

"I thought they tried to screen your type out in advance," I said. "Or is the mesh in Steel City just too coarse?"

"Take it easy, Sherlock," Donovan said. "There's a few routine questions."

"You ask them," I said.

"How long was Traven here with you?"

"About forty-five minutes."

"Of course you would of called and turned him in when you got around to it."

"No," I said. "I was going to take him to Steel City and line up a lawyer for him and let the lawyer turn him in."

"How'd he happen to come to you in the first place?" asked the Sergeant.

I looked at Donovan and he sighed and repeated the question.

"A friend of his referred him. A Peter Bowman."

The Sergeant got slowly on his feet.

"Peter Bowman the attorney?" he said.

"Lieutenant," I said, "will you explain to the great white hunter that I am very sick to my stomach and that if I have to talk to him I may have an accident?"

Every man has a brink. This was the Sergeant's. On the way over it he caught a piece of my coat in his fist and crowded me against the wall. He had the wounded animal look again.

"I'll arrange a free nose-cleaning for you," he rumbled, "any time you want to come to town."

"Lieutenant," I said, "either look the other way or tell him to let go."

"Break it up," Donovan said.

The Sergeant hung on for a minute, bruising my ribs with his knuckles, manipulating a white scar that ran from his left nostril to his left ear and disappeared in his sideburn. He was a shade on the dandy side and, except for the scar, his face hadn't been spoiled yet. I wound one up to perform this service for him, but Donovan pushed between us and he let go. I walked away, shaking the twist out of my coat.

"Get him out of here," I said. "He's without jurisdiction and without a warrant. If he's got questions, tell him I'll gladly testify at his hearing."

He scowled, but I guess it had finally dribbled down to him that he was not among friends. Donovan showed him the simple mechanism of the doorknob.

"You must be tired, Sergeant," he said. "I'll be along."

He went. I heard him going all the way to his car.

I offered Donovan a drink and he turned it down.

"You're gettin' kind of lippy lately," he said.

"Murder makes me sick."

"It's true," he said, "that Traven had a gun."

"Maybe. But the Sergeant couldn't see that from where you were and Traven wasn't running."

"You know how it is, a guy gets nervous—"

"Not every guy. You never got that nervous in your life."

"Maybe I'm too dumb to get nervous."

If he thought he could draw me into a provocation, he had some more thinking to do. And he could do it when the need arose. "Answer me a question," I said.

"I don't know."

"How did the Steel City cops get here so soon? They shoot them out of cannons?"

"You don't give the police any credit at all, do you? It don't take a jab in the butt to get them started."

I waited and pretty soon he said, "They were already in town."

"What brought 'em?"

"They got a tip, a phone call."

"From Peter Bowman?"

"They don't know who."

"Are they trying to find out?"

"Maybe. But the way they told it to me, they had a perfect case against Traven."

"Good for them."

He went to the door and took off his hat and fooled with it. "Any more questions?" he asked.

"Just one. Who wanted him dead, instead of on trial?"

He put his hat on.

"I don't know. I'll ask the Sergeant. So long, you poor man's Pinkerton."

"So long, copper."

I sat there at the desk until the sound of his heavy tread had faded, till the car door had slammed and the wheels swished out of hearing. I sat there a while longer. I took out one of the snapshots of the naked girl and looked at it. A small, fragile girl, not very pretty, with short, light-colored hair and high, little nonfunctional breasts. There was a faint forced smile on her pixie-like face.

She might have been fifteen, or then again twenty-five or thirty. It looked as if someone had caught her coming out of the shower.

I put the snapshot in my wallet, wasted a call on my answering service and looked up "Bowman, Peter, Atty." in the telephone book.

CHAPTER FOUR

It was one of the old homes near Diversey Parkway and Clark Street. It had recently been remodeled and newly landscaped and it had cost considerably more than a young corporation lawyer could afford. A new Eldorado stood on the drive.

I rang three times and a woman opened the door. When I told her my name, she reached for me impulsively, then stepped back and beckoned me inside.

"I'm Karen Lloyd Bowman," she said. "My husband is upstairs. I'll call him."

It was easy to look at her. At her full height, she was shorter than I, but not much. Her skin was very white in contrast to her black hair and she had big brown eyes, faintly restless. Her figure was full and womanly and she was tall enough to carry it; and her mouth was vividly red in her white face.

"I'm glad you came," she said. "Pete's nearly beside himself. Did Chuck Traven find you?"

"To his eternal regret," I said.

"What happened?"

"He decided to run," I said. "Maybe it wasn't a bad idea. By then the cops were there, though, and one of them shot him."

She shook her head slightly and her brown eyes blinked slowly.

"He shouldn't have tried it. Sooner or later—"

"Yes, ma'am," I said.

She gestured.

"Please sit down," she said. "I'll get Pete." She shook her head again. "I don't know how he'll take it. They were very close friends."

"We can't know till we try," I said.

"I'll get him."

She moved slowly to the stairs and started climbing. I managed to get my eyes off her at the fifth step. But she stuck in my mind like an after-image. Something about her, in name and bearing, rang a distant bell.

It was a large room, traditionally and expensively furnished. On a massive coffee table were an ice hamper, a half-full whisky bottle and a couple of wet glasses. Through an open door at one side, I could see into a dimly lighted study or den. Innocuous music peeled off the FM band of a hidden radio.

The stairs creaked in a genteel way and Mrs. Bowman was descending with a young man in slacks and a sports jacket. He halted on the steps, gazing at me. His wife looked back at him from one end of a king-sized sofa and he came on down, somewhat in the manner of a dog on leash.

"This is my husband, Pete Bowman, Mr.—"

"Call me Mac," I said. "I'm used to it."

Bowman and I shook hands. His was clammy.

"Your friend Traven was shot to death by a Sergeant Downs from Steel City," I said.

He stared at me openmouthed, his head shaking in disbelief.

"Have a drink, dear," Mrs. Bowman said.

He sat down beside her and accepted the drink she had mixed. He was on the chubby side with a florid complexion and an expression that at seventeen must have seemed cherubic and carefree but now, at twenty-nine or thirty, looked like a jaded life-of-the-party mask that would change little in the next forty years.

"Chuck wouldn't run," he said. "He wasn't like that."

"Anybody's like that sometimes," I said.

"They were very close friends," his wife said. "Army friends, in Korea. You know how that is."

"He saved my life once," Bowman said. "We were out on this patrol—cold, Jesus! We'd been out two, three hours—"

"I don't think Mac requires all the details," Mrs. Bowman said. "He saved your life. He was very brave."

Bowman drooped and held his peace and the glass. A muscle was jumping in my throat. His wife built him another drink and pretty soon he managed to straighten out a few things—not without some help.

He told me he was an attorney—his wife explained he was with a Chicago firm handling some large estates.

He told me Traven had called him in the late afternoon and said he was in trouble.

Mrs. Bowman cut in, speaking more precisely. "He said his wife had been murdered and he didn't know who had done it and he was frightened."

"Yes," Bowman said, "and I couldn't think of anything except that he ought to go to somebody with practical experience—some sort of—"

"He thought of you," Mrs. Bowman said.

She rose abruptly and pushed through a swinging door into a kitchen. When she came back there was a clean glass in her hand.

"Sorry, I forgot my manners. Drink, Mac?"

"With water, please," I said.

"I guess it was an imposition," Bowman said, "just to send him cold like that—"

"We should have called you first," his wife said.

I tasted my drink and re-crossed my legs.

"After you sent him to me," I said, "what made you decide to call the police?"

His face flushed deeply.

"Well," he said, "we talked it over—you understand it was quite a shock, reading about it in the paper—"

She came to his rescue.

"We weren't sure he'd follow through," she said. "We were afraid that if he just wandered around the city aimlessly, anything might happen."

"Well," I said, "he followed through all right."

Bowman held out his empty glass and his wife took care of it for him.

"What hurts," he said, "is that I might have prevented the whole thing. If I had only called him—"

"What he means to say," his wife put in, "is that we were in Steel City yesterday and we might have called Chuck. Pete was on business and I was visiting my father."

I was looking at Bowman.

"Doesn't he ever get to finish his own sentence?" I said.

She ground out her cigarette, sat back in her seat and concentrated on her drink. Bowman shifted uncomfortably.

"Well, now," he said, "Karen's upset—"

"I'm not upset," she said, "but possibly we've kept Mr.—Mac—long enough."

I had never before been thrown out of such a nice place so graciously and it made me a little giddy. I had to reach twice for my hat. Mrs. Bowman's face reflected a quiet scorn that got under my skin in spite of the fact I had asked for it. I made a point of meeting her eyes.

"Something just came through to me," I said. "You're Calvin Lloyd's daughter. The Green Acres Lloyd."

She nodded stiffly.

"You're a brilliant detective," she said.

I nodded good night. Bowman went to the door with me and I got him outside.

"I'm sorry," he mumbled, "we've been upset—"

I took out my wallet.

"Forget it," I said. "I just thought, since you had sent him around, I ought to report."

I handed him the snapshot of the naked girl.

"Traven gave me this," I said. "It doesn't mean anything to me. You might want to have it—or to throw it away."

He stared at the picture, holding it up to catch the faint light from the door lamp. I couldn't see his face well enough to read it. "Thanks," he said. "Thanks for trying."

"I'm sorry about your friend."

"Well—" he said, "good night."

I went away quickly.

* * * *

Shortly after midnight, less than an hour from the time I had left him, he knocked on my door. I hadn't bothered to go to bed.

CHAPTER FIVE

He was alone, and when I opened the door he looked at me with the deceptive lucidity of deep drunkenness.

"Thing keeps disturbing me," he said. "While the police were shooting Chuck, where were you?"

I looked at his over-bright eyes, fixed on me with alcoholic stubbornness.

"I wasn't holding him," I said, "if that's what you mean. Come on in."

"This Lieutenant—Donovan? What kind of a cop is he?"

So he had picked up a few details, probably on a late news broadcast.

"Let me put it this way," I said. "If you were in bad trouble and a policeman was the only man who could help you, Donovan would be the one you'd want."

He didn't want to give over, but the stuff had caught up with him and he went slack. I nudged him to the couch and he sank down and held his head in both hands. I put my feet on the desk and waited for him to look up.

"Is it just Traven," I said, "that's chewing on you?"

"Honest, I don't know."

The combination of alcohol and exhaustion had thickened his voice. I couldn't always make out the words.

"He was such a sweet guy, Traven. He was my sergeant in Korea. Whatever you think now, I wasn't a bad officer, five, six years ago—"

"I believe it."

"After we got home, we banged around Steel City. I was finishing up law school and he was studying drafting, nights. There was a crowd of us, you know? Kind of a last big ball before we settled down. Used to go to the Tropical Gardens, a dance hall—"

"Traven mentioned it to me."

"It was a new experience for me. I'd been brought up—well, what I was, I was a so-called rich kid. Then my old man kind of flipped and lost everything and—aah, the hell with it."

"That girl he married—Connie," I said.

"Connie Waters." His face went into his hands again. "She's going to keep coming up!"

"I'm not pushing you to talk about it."

He groped for a cigarette, found one, and I lit it for him. His face in the match glow was haggard and sick.

"I played around with her," he said. "I was pretty good at playing around. Not any more though. Scared of my wife."

I passed that one.

"Anyway," he said, "I never saw Connie after I married Karen."

"Never heard from her?"

"No." He raised his head and looked at me strangely. "Come to think of it, that's kind of funny too. She might have—" He dropped it in mid-air and I let it float to the ground, then picked it up and played with it awhile.

"She had something on you?" I asked.

"What woman hasn't, on somebody? Sure she did, with pictures."

"Well, they wouldn't be much use to her if you weren't married at the time, unless you were going to run for public office."

"No, I guess not."

"Did Traven know about what she had on you?"

"Maybe not about the pictures. He knew what she was like. God knows, I warned him. When he said he was going to marry her, I couldn't believe it. I pleaded with him! I wish—" His hands were shaking and he held them out from his face, staring at them. I had to decide whether to offer the drink he needed, in the hope it would brace him, or to withhold it and use his need as the lever to pry up my own.

I got down a bottle and glass, but stopped short of him, holding them out of reach.

"To get back to the pictures," I said, "for instance, the one I gave you—" Blinking at the bottle, he reached into his pocket and brought out the snapshot. The telephone rang, a devil's shriek in the quiet room. Bowman jumped so the couch springs rattled. I jumped a little myself.

I handed him the bottle and glass and got to the phone at the third ring. En route, I made a paper profit at ten to one on the identity of the caller.

"…Yes, Mrs. Bowman, he's with me."

"I just wanted to make sure he's all right."

I glanced at Bowman and he gazed at me benignly, holding the bottle in one hand, the glass, three fingers full, in the other.

"Would you like to speak to him?" I asked.

Bowman shook his head briskly.

"Not necessarily," Mrs. Bowman said. "Just so someone will see him home safely."

"Of course," I said. "Personally."

"Thanks," she said.

"Not at all."

Bowman waved the bottle at me.

"Remarkable woman," he said. "All I am or hope to be. Comes from great stock—Calvin Lloyd, the Sire of Green Acres. Must bring no shame on Green Acres. Must conduct oneself in the proper manner. Never sully the name of Calvin Lloyd—people lose faith—whole thing collapses. Am I right?"

"Whatever you say," I said. "About the picture—"

"Nothing. A bagatelle."

He leveled on me with the bottle, scowling darkly.

"Indiscretion of my youth," he said. "Connie, not the picture—" It trailed off and he seemed to lose the thread. But when I tried to pick it up for him, he started in again, unable to tolerate any more interruption.

"You should have taken care of Chuck, you know. You goofed. Now you try to make out it was my fault. You think I turned him in. Maybe you think I killed Connie myself—let Chuck take the blame."

He had a death grip on the bottle neck and I decided it would be easier to get him home after he passed out, which he would certainly do before long. He was in the crying stage now.

"Such a sweet guy, Traven. And they shot him. Over a bitch like Connie—"

"Not exactly. Connie was already dead."

Tears streamed down his pink face.

"Marianne—" he said chokingly. "What'll become of poor Marianne?"

The hair bristled on the back of my neck.

"Who?" I said.

"Marianne," he mumbled. "Girl used to hang around. Poor, scrawny little kid—"

"Who was she? What was she to Connie?"

"I don't know—Connie was sort of a guardian for her—some guardian—"

"What was her full name?"

"McLeod. Marianne McLeod. Strange kid—"

I wrote it down. He didn't seem to notice. He fumbled around and came up with the snapshot. The tears still showed on his face, but he had the flow under control.

"Connie framed her—kid was taking a shower. Connie called her, pretended she was hurt, something. Marianne didn't know I was there. She came running out and Connie took her picture with a flash camera, just as she stood there. Dirty damn trick."

"She was just a kid you say?"

"Fifteen, sixteen. That was the last night I ever saw Connie."

"You never fooled around with Marianne?"

"Hell, no!"

"Because that would be something she would really have on you."

He registered high indignation.

"I never touched the girl!"

"Why would Traven tell me he didn't know her, if Connie was her guardian?"

"No legal guardian, like that, just looked after her—mother just died—"

"So maybe Traven really didn't know her."

"If he said so, it's true. Such a sweet guy—"

"Do you think he killed his wife?"

The blunt question had an unexpected sobering effect. He drew himself up and put himself together. The process resembled the over-expressive squeezing of a concertina.

"Certainly not," he said.

"Somebody did. You realize what it means, if it wasn't Traven? Somebody was watching him, close enough to know he came to Chicago. Either he was framed, or by coincidence put himself in a position to be used. I'll have to say, he co-operated with dazzling success."

"What do you mean?"

"He did everything wrong. He handled everything in sight with his bare hands. He didn't call the police or even a doctor. He let in the neighbors. Then he ran out. If somebody else did it, then Traven was a heaven-sent miracle."

Bowman's eyes had lost their vagueness.

"Suppose he had done everything right," he said. "Would you figure him more likely innocent?"

It was a hard-hitting question with a built-in answer. Bowman started the climb to his feet. I got up to help but he pushed me away and walked to the desk, not without dignity. He was getting to be quite a guy. I wondered whether the drunk act had been planned, to feel me out.

He was pulling money from his wallet.

"I've got five hundred dollars," he said, "says Chuck Traven didn't kill his wife."

"I can't match it," I said.

"Don't mean you to. What's your customary retainer?"

He threw some bills on my desk.

"Whoa," I said. "The police are already making an investigation—"

"But they'll stop now."

He was right, of course.

"Maybe it would be better to close the door on it," I said. "If we get close to the real killer and he gets nervous, you can't predict—"

"You weren't closing the door on it when you gave me that picture of Marianne McLeod."

"I just thought you might like to have it."

He scooped up the bills and pressed them on me.

"Keep thinking," he said. "Even if he's dead, he deserves to have a clear name."

"That's worth money to you?"

"I told you, he saved my life."

I found an envelope, put the money in it and sealed it. I wrote his name on it and the amount and dropped it into a locking drawer.

"If you change your mind," I said, "the money's here for you. No questions."

As I crossed the room to get my hat, I was marveling at his recovery. With my back to him, I asked, "How did you get here?" He didn't answer, and when I turned he was mumbling something I couldn't hear.

"I'll take you home," I said.

He nodded agreeably, took two steps toward the door and fell on his face.

* * * *

I had him on my shoulder when Karen Bowman opened the door. She didn't say a word while I followed her up the long stairs and down a hall to his bedroom. It was plainly furnished, masculine and in good order.

He was quite a load and we worked both sides of the bed getting him laid out. I was pulling off his shoes when Mrs. Bowman, near the head of the bed, brushed hard against the telephone stand. It rattled fiercely and there was a light thud on the floor. She made a small sound and I thought she had hurt herself. But when I got around there, she was staring down at a small package. It was maybe five inches square and an inch thick, brown wrapping paper tied with ribbon.

"Darling," she said, "a present for me? And you didn't even mention it."

Pete was oblivious. Slowly she bent and picked up the package. I thought that if it was a present, the store had got the wrapping paper from an old, dusty shelf. She began loosening the ribbon and I turned to pull a blanket over Pete. When I looked at her again, she was standing very stiff with her eyes closed, the rumpled paper on the package pressed tight against her breast. I waited a minute, then said, "I guess he'll do for now."

She opened her eyes and blinked them at me. She was wearing a tailored white dressing gown, belted in gold, and her black hair was on her shoulders. I couldn't help thinking how easily the combination of her beauty and social background could drive even a very stout fellow to drink.

She glanced again at Pete, then, clutching the package, walked out of the room and downstairs. I had said good night and was at the door when she called me back, her voice muted, froggy.

"Mac, am I really that sort of person, the kind you made me out?"

"How did I insult you?"

"It was the way you looked at me, and that remark about Pete's not getting to finish a sentence."

"Oh, that—"

"Maybe if you knew Pete better. He can be wonderful fun, but he's shaky in a crisis. I guess I've developed the habit of taking charge."

"I'm not a domestic relations counselor, Mrs. Bowman," I said. "If I can help in any other way, just let me know."

Upstairs a door banged. Her eyes shifted.

"Karen—?"

I could hear him making his way along the hall.

"Karen—" he called again.

"Yes, dear?"

He appeared at the top of the stairs in shirt sleeves and stocking feet, clinging to the rail.

"I hired Mac," he said firmly, "to look into the Traven thing. I've given him a retainer."

"All right, Pete," she said calmly.

"Just wanted you to know."

"As you wish, dear," she said.

He clung there, weaving noticeably, and for a few moments the odds were even as to whether he would stay on his feet or fall down the stairs. But the brief act of self-assertion must have steeled him because he turned and made it all right going away to bed.

Karen drew a long, slow breath and tossed her thick hair with one hand. Her face was curiously empty.

"Pete gave you money," she said, "to investigate Connie Traven's murder?"

"As he told you."

"You know the condition he was in."

"The money he gave me is in a sealed envelope, pending sober agreement."

"Do you have a minute?"

Without waiting for an answer, she turned, and I followed her across the room to the den. She closed the door silently, indicated a chair and sat down on a love seat, facing me. The partially open package was on her lap now.

"We told you we were in Steel City yesterday," she said. I nodded. "We drove over together, but came back separately. Pete dropped me off at Green Acres and went on into town. I didn't see him again till late that night."

I waited awhile and she pulled the wrapping paper away and handed me the contents of the package. There was no surprise in it for me now. If she was disappointed, it didn't show.

It was pretty routine stuff. There were half a dozen letters in scented envelopes, addressed to Miss Constance Waters in Steel City. The return address in each case was "No. 48, North Drive, Pine Lake."

I didn't bother to read the letters. In addition to them there were eight photographs, the same size as those of Marianne McLeod and of about that quality. The lady who had participated in the posing was unknown to me by sight and could as well have been Connie Traven as anyone. In a stiff brown folder were eight negatives to match the prints. I couldn't be positive that they were originals.

I adjusted the packet in the same order as when she had given it to me and replaced it on her lap. She watched me steadily.

"I knew these existed," she said. "I'm a modern woman. I understand about wild oats and most of the facts of life—although one of these I just can't believe, even when I see it."

"How did you know about them?"

"Pete told me, long ago. We laughed about it. It was in the past. Now it's in the present, suddenly, and how did he come by them?"

I shrugged.

"He talked her out of them, or bought them."

She shook her head firmly.

"I knew too much about her to believe the first. And I know how much money is available to Pete in cash that he can get hold of without my knowing."

"All right," I said, "then what do you think?"

"I don't think about it at all," she said. "I don't want to. I don't want anybody else to think about it, especially you."

I sat there for a minute and she said, "How much does it cost to keep you from thinking?"

I restrained an impulse to laugh at her.

"Leaving aside the moral issue—" I said.

"For an American wife protecting her home," she said, "there's only one issue, and you're an honorable man."

I got on my feet.

"We're getting a little fancy," I said. "What are you going to do with that stuff?"

"I'm going to put it where I found it and keep an eye on it. When Pete sobers up, he'll destroy it. If he doesn't, I will."

"Good idea," I said, "if you'll excuse me—" I got hold of the doorknob and she pushed the package aside and got up. Her fingers fluttered at the fastening of her belt.

"What kind of a deal would you make?" she asked.

I shook my head.

"I'll give you this and it's all I have," I said. "If I do any thinking about the Traven affair, it won't be on Pete's time."

There was a fifteen-second period of silence. Then she said very softly, "All right, Mister Detective. Hop to it."

She stayed where she was and I let myself out. I had mixed feelings of regret at leaving her and relief at being alone. The cold drive to my office did nothing to resolve them.

* * * *

They were far from resolved at noon the next day when I met Pete Bowman for lunch. I found him in a Loop bar and grill, crowded, steamy and noisy. We had to wait fifteen minutes for a table in a back corner. Pete was sober, but shaky and pale. Happily he didn't waste much time on apologies for the previous night, which he seemed to remember clearly.

"You read this morning's paper?" he said.

"Uh-huh. They're closing the case."

With as much conviction as I had ever heard in a man's voice, he said, "Chuck Traven did not kill his wife."

"Maybe."

"I think we can prove it."

I finished my sandwich, brought out the envelope with his money in it and laid it on the table.

"I don't think so," I said.

He picked up the envelope and turned it over a couple of times. "You mean you're backing out?" he said.

"If you have to put it that way."

"But why? I'm not drunk now, Mac."

"I find I just can't undertake the assignment at this time."

"If you need more money—"

"No!"

He saw I was getting hot and laid off. We finished our beer.

"If you had gone ahead with it," he said, "what were you going to do first?"

"I was going to find Marianne McLeod."

"How would you have gone about it?"

"I would probably hire help. There are skip tracers in town who can find anybody, even if they're hiding out."

"Skip tracers. Would you have to tell them why you wanted the information?"

"No—" It dawned on me where he was heading. "Pete, don't get any ideas. It's not for amateurs."

He put the money away in his pocket.

"Thanks," he said. "The only advice I never follow is the kind you get for nothing."

"All right," I said. "You buy the lunch."

I got up and he said, "One more thing. Last night after I went to bed, did you hang around and talk to Karen?"

I looked at his pink cherub's face and felt some pity for him. It felt bad.

"If I did," I said, "it was only talk, and if I should tell you about it, all it would amount to would be more free advice. So long, Pete."

He didn't try to detain me. I went home and reread the piece in the paper that told how the Steel City police had wrapped up the Traven case. I read it half a dozen times and finally I made myself believe it, the way you come to believe something because even if it isn't true, there's nothing you can do about it.

And it might have ended there, with the thing neatly stashed on the top shelf and everybody getting his proper sleep. Only, three nights later, another thing happened.

CHAPTER SIX

It was Donovan on the phone and eight o'clock at night.

"Party goin' on out South," he said. "Meet me downtown in twenty minutes."

He hung up and I had no choice. I picked up a cab across the street and we made it to headquarters in nineteen minutes. Donovan was in the back seat of his official car and the door hung open. I managed to scramble aboard before we got into the street. There were the two of us in back and a uniformed driver up front. He was in a hell of a hurry. Donovan shouted over the screaming siren.

"What're you doin' on the Traven case?"

"Nothing!" I yelled. "It's closed." The siren faded unexpectedly and I was still yelling. "What are *you* doing about it?"

He looked at me with some surprise.

"Nothin' for me to do," he said. "It belongs to the Steel City people."

Then he let me sit there. If I had been touted off on how far we had to go, I'd have packed a lunch. We traversed all there was of Lake Shore Drive southward, then jogged and angled off toward Blue Island. The traffic thinned and we laid off the siren. Donovan pulled a cigar out of his pocket, stripped off the wrapper, chewed off the end and spit it out the window and got the thing going. It was a high-class cigar and I wondered who had given it to him.

"Remember Deacon Roberts?" he said.

I remembered.

"Then you remember that one night, while the Deacon was removing the cash money from somebody else's safe, his two accomplices scragged the night watchman. I had the honor of bringing them in."

"I remember," I said.

"On account of the Deacon being smart enough to turn in his two helpers, they drew life and he got off with five to ten for the robbery. Seemed like a good deal all around."

There was something about the tone of his voice.

"Well," he went on, "the Deacon was always a model prisoner, so naturally he wouldn't stay locked up for long. He got out a month ago."

The siren went up as the driver bulled his way through a traffic jam. We waited it out.

"That's the way it goes," Donovan said, "the guy is in, then he's out. His nose is clean, we don't bother him. Then a while ago, on account of this thing comin' up, I put in a call and freshened up on the make we had on the Deacon."

"Somebody got to him?" I said.

"He ain't dead yet."

"Go ahead."

"At the time he knocked over that safe, he was shacked up in Steel City with a lady named Anita McLeod. She must of known somethin' about the caper, because just before the Deacon's trial, they got married."

We braked sharply, skidding, and I put my feet hard against the rest.

"This McLeod woman had a daughter, eleven, twelve years old, name of Marianne. Besides her, there was another girl livin' with 'em at the time—a Connie Waters, later known as Connie Traven. As we know, she is now dead of murder."

Though we were now rolling smoothly, I kept pushing with my feet. The car drifted to a stop in front of a brick building adjoining a precinct station. A blue neon light over the door read: EMERGENCY HOSPITAL.

"I guess this is it," Donovan said.

* * * *

It may be that the recent white Anglo-Saxon Christian struggle to canonize the informer will be lost in the rivers and back streets of America, where "rat" is still spelled with three letters and the only way to save your life is to lose it. The thing about a code, whether you go for its objectives or not, is that it works. When it stops working, it stops being a code. This particular code of which we are speaking was still working in a cluttered alley on the deep South Side.

William "Deacon" Roberts, forty-eight years old, mild-mannered, soft-spoken, with sensitive fingers and an encyclopedic knowledge of metallurgy, tensile strengths and vault engineering, had tried to pretend the code would stop working for him. And all he had got for his trouble was the point of a knife in his heart and, I doubted not, a somewhat more sizable crowd at his passing than he could ever have drawn for a legitimate demonstration of his craft.

They had made him as comfortable as possible. A doctor was leaning over him with a stethoscope when Donovan and I checked in past the guard at the door. We waited awhile and the doctor shook his head and spoke in a low monotone.

"…about all we could do. I doubt if he has a chance. I think he can talk, but take it easy."

Donovan nodded and went to the bed. Roberts was stripped to the waist. A couple of wide bands of adhesive tape showed on his left ribs. He looked gaunt and wasted, with thin hair straggling over his forehead. Donovan spoke to him quietly and he roused and opened his eyes. His mental faculties seemed intact. If he had pain, he didn't show it.

"Lieutenant," he said. "Sorry to cause trouble."

"Okay, Deacon," Donovan said. "Who stuck you?"

"I don't know."

"Come on, this is no time to hold out. Tell me who it was. I'll fry him."

"Some punk, Lieutenant. An amateur. Jumped me from behind."

"You think he was hired? Those two you helped put away?"

"This punk—no. Listen, will you do something—"

"Give me more description," Donovan cut in. "Dark, light, tall, short—"

Roberts lifted his hand.

"Forget it, Lieutenant. I got a favor to ask."

Donovan stood back and studied him, as if to estimate his staying power, then did what he had to do.

"You're on a two-way line," he said. "You help me, I'll help you."

Roberts closed his eyes and turned away. I moved in closer behind Donovan.

"I don't know," he said slowly, "medium size. Dark, I guess. Couldn't see his face much—"

"Did he say anything?"

"Yeah—" I glanced at the door as if the doctor ought, by telepathy, to know he was wanted. "He said—'You came to the wrong place, mister.' I started to turn around and he ducked and hit me."

"What about his voice?"

"Just a voice—a punk's voice."

"What did he mean by 'the wrong place'?"

"I don't know."

"Did he mean that woman you called on—Mrs. Carmichael?"

"Honest, I don't know."

"What did you want from Mrs. Carmichael?"

"Just—information—" Something hurt him badly and he tried to roll over. Donovan gave him a hand and he rolled slowly onto his side and blinked at the wall.

"Did you get the information?" Donovan said.

"No. She didn't know about it."

"What was the information?"

His eyes blinked slowly, fully. Open, they were too big for his face. I wondered what he was really looking at.

"Not much time, Lieutenant," he said. "About that favor—"

"Okay," Donovan said. "Whatever I can do."

"My stepdaughter—Anita McLeod's girl, Marianne. Works an all-night hash house in Steel City. Did a little time for shoplifting. Very bum beef—just a kid—" His voice trailed off and I headed for the door, but it opened and the doctor came in with a syringe. While he went through the ministrations, he muttered to Donovan.

"Better talk fast. This'll knock him out for a couple of hours—or a lot longer."

The doctor left and Donovan said, "About the girl, Deacon—" Roberts pushed himself awake.

"Anita had money—quite a lot—came in regular. Never would talk about it. Kept it in a bank, in cash. Said it was for Marianne."

He went away again.

"Deacon—?" Donovan prompted, his broad fingers massaging the wasted neck. "Hey, Deacon—" He came back, but I had to come out in the open and bend close in order to hear. He blinked those big eyes at me.

"Anita was all right," he muttered, "kind of stupid, but okay—a good cook. The kid was about twelve when I met her—built like a pencil—" It was a gruesome thought, but I knew that a man can reminisce himself to death. I made words with my mouth at Donovan and he shook the Deacon lightly.

"About Connie Waters," he said sharply. "Did you know Connie Waters?"

"Kid ought to get a break," Roberts said. "She don't know about the money—where it is. I tried to find it—split with her—maybe Anita buried it someplace, about what she'd do... the kid's all right, pretty sharp—" Whatever he was looking at now was not in the room with us. His eyelids had puckered raggedly so that his eyes no longer dominated his face.

"Connie Waters," Donovan repeated.

The eyes blinked.

"A cheap twist—after my time mostly—I knew her some. Operator. Moved in when I went up last time—" The doctor came again with his stethoscope and some other equipment, including a nurse. They worked over him for three or four minutes. The nurse went away, the doctor stayed. They had put him on his back again and his gray face was slack and empty. But when Donovan spoke, his eyes opened and he seemed lucid enough.

"Lieutenant," he said, "do something for the kid, huh?"

They looked at each other for quite a long time, each on his own side of a fence that would collapse very soon and for the rest of time.

"Sure," Donovan said. He gestured to me and I stepped up beside him. "Mac—you ever meet the Deacon?" He made the introduction. Roberts swiveled his eyes to take me in. His head moved.

"Glad to meet you," he said. "Excuse me if I don't get up."

"Sure," I said.

He closed his eyes and pretty soon his breathing had changed: long, deep surges with increasing intervals between, so that after each one, I waited what seemed forever for the next. The doctor moved in quickly and did something. Roberts' head turned restlessly and his mouth fluttered.

"Marianne—" he said.

"Yeah, Deacon?" Donovan said.

But this time when he went away, there was no provision for the return trip. We waited for him to draw another long breath, but he never did. Maybe he had wanted to, but by then it had been too late.

"That's it," the doctor said. "Who was he, Lieutenant?"

We were leaving the room. Donovan's voice was gruffer than usual. His big hand massaged the door handle.

"It don't matter now," he said. "So long, Doc."

* * * *

I stood outside with Donovan. He kicked a discarded milk can into the gutter.

"I got to go talk to a lady that probably don't know nothin' about this and she'll get all upset."

"This is the city," I said. "You're a cop."

He shifted his shoulders under his coat.

"Want to string along?" he said.

"I guess my ride home depends on it."

We walked over in front of the precinct station and got into his car.

CHAPTER SEVEN

It was a walk-up apartment at the third floor rear. There were the mingled odors of old wood, dusty carpeting and whatever pungent treats the tenants had eaten two, three hours earlier. It was drab and respectable and, at a glance, fitting in every way to the woman who opened the door to us. Her name, in Old English script on an engraved card in a brass frame, had read: "*Mrs. Lilian Carmichael.*"

Donovan twisted his face into the gargoyle mask you could take for a smile if you had to, and hit the blarney trail.

"I can see that an honest, law-abidin' girl like yourself has nothin' to hide. But this is part of my job, ma'am, and you wouldn't want me to lose that now, would you?"

Corny, but it rarely failed. Mrs. Carmichael let down the chain and opened up.

Thirty, maybe, she had honey-blond hair that was clean but lacked gloss. It was cut and dressed wrong for her, short and straight and pinned back on both sides of her squarish face. She was of medium height, big boned and not fat, with good breasts; only, I thought, if she had to put a harness on them, it should lift up rather than bear down. She wore hexagonal, rimless glasses with plain gold bows that accentuated the jut of her brow. She wore no visible cosmetics. It's a matter of taste and a woman has a right to put small stock in physical loveliness, but I thought Mrs. Carmichael might have practiced with less diligence.

She offered us seats side by side on a sofa as unyielding as a church pew. I visualized her sleeping on a bed of nails, alone, naturally.

She sat across from us, nearer Donovan, in a matching wing chair, her knees and ankles together and her hands folded on the square platform her knees made. Her fingers were white and clean and there was a film of neutral polish on her neatly trimmed nails. She watched Donovan with a detached calm. She didn't look at me at all.

"I've already told the officers everything I know," she said.

Donovan nodded.

"Yes, ma'am. Your husband's not here, Mrs. Carmichael?"

She had clear blue eyes that rarely blinked. But if they were the windows of her soul, they were the one-way type. She could see out, but I couldn't see in.

"We're divorced," she said. "I haven't seen him for three years."

Donovan sighed with what I knew to be relief. He was always a little worried about his honor, and with cause. Some of the bribes he had been offered by desperate ladies would make your hair stand on end.

"Does he pay you any alimony?" he asked.

"No, I've always worked."

"Where, ma'am?"

"The Second National Bank. My branch is just around the corner on Third Street."

Donovan was all sweet Irish approval.

"Takes good honest people to run banks," he said. "What department are you in, Mrs. Carmichael?"

"I'm just a clerk. Most of my work is in the safe deposit section."

"Oh—like if I get a box, I come in and you're the girl that tells me to sign my name and takes a key and you go in the vault with me to open up."

"That's about it," she said. "Of course, I have other duties."

"Sure. How long did you know that poor fella they picked up in the alley?"

"I never saw him before tonight. He said his name was Roberts."

"Just come up and knock on the door, did he?"

"Yes. He wanted to know about someone—some Scotch name—McLean—McKay—"

"McLeod maybe? Could it have been McLeod?"

"I think so. Yes."

In the wall toward the rear of the building were two doors: one swinging type to the kitchen; the other would lead to a hallway, bedroom and bath. Both doors were closed.

"What did he want to know, ma'am?" Donovan asked.

"Something about money that belonged to this McLeod woman. I knew nothing about it."

She unlaced her fingers, smoothed at her tight suit skirt and laced them up again. Against the wall between the kitchen and bedroom doors was a spindly-legged desk with a slanted front that would let down. Beside the desk was a telephone stand. She had one of those office number finders with the flip top.

"When you couldn't give him the information," Donovan said, "he went away?"

"Well—eventually."

Beside the sofa was an ash tray on wrought-iron legs. There were half a dozen cigarette butts in it.

"Oh," Donovan said. "He come in for a while?"

"Naturally I asked him in. I didn't expect him to stay. He seemed lonely. He smoked several cigarettes."

"What did he talk about?"

"He just sort of rambled. He told me he'd been away for a long time and the last he had seen her, she had mentioned this money—"

"Did he say where he'd been away to?"

"No. I thought he meant in some other country."

Donovan stared gloomily at his hands.

"Who was he?" she said. "The police seemed to know him—"

"Yeah," Donovan said. "Called him 'The Deacon' He was a crook, ma'am. A safecracker."

She blinked, right on schedule. If she had emotions, she kept them in one of her safe deposit boxes.

"He seemed so nice," she said, "so gentle."

"Oh, he was a very nice fella," Donovan said. "I never had nothin' against him except he kept dippin' in the wrong tills."

She lowered her eyes in a formal way.

"I'm sorry he died so violently," she said.

Donovan looked at his watch.

"When he finally decided to go, how did he do it?"

"How? He walked—I don't know what you—"

"Did he just get up and walk away?"

"He went out the back way, if that's what you mean?"

"I guess it is."

"He said it would be a short cut to his car."

"You showed him out by the rear?"

"Yes."

"And what happened next?"

"We stood on the porch for a minute and he apologized for taking my time. I said I hoped he'd find what he wanted. Then he said good night and started down the steps. I came back inside."

"Uh-huh."

"It must have been about ten minutes later—I heard shouting. I ran out on the porch. There were two or three people down there and I saw a man lying in the alley—"

"Roberts?"

"I couldn't tell. Someone yelled at me, something about calling the police."

"So you came in and did that?"

"Yes. I didn't really think about it. I just acted automatically." She was hating herself for it. She was a careful, rational woman for whom "acting automatically" or on impulse—any impulse—would be in the nature of sinning.

"You're a good, strong woman," Donovan said. "Will you show me how you let him out, the back way?"

"Certainly. It's this way, through the kitchen."

She rose primly and Donovan got up to follow. He didn't look at me, so I stayed where I was. The door opened and shut with a light clatter. I heard their footsteps on the linoleum.

I walked over to the slim-legged desk and pulled at the slanted cover. It was locked. I pushed the little spring at the bottom of the pop-up list finder and it opened to the "Ps." In neat, precise lettering, the word "Police" was followed by the emergency number of the local precinct. Indented below it were the words: "Chicago—Hqs." and another number. So she had that covered.

I closed the finder, slid the separator up to "F" and flipped it again. Sure enough, there was "Fire" and the number. I slid the separator to the top and started with the "As." There were some names that meant nothing to me. "Acme Cleaners" was crossed out. I wondered what had gone wrong there.

The "B" page was nearly full. It started with the main heading "Bank" and there were eight or ten subheads under that. There was a name, "Bertha's," which I took to be a beauty shop. There were some others. Toward the bottom was the name "Bowman, P.," and a number.

I went on through the book quickly and found nothing else familiar. Several pages were blank. On the floor, half under the desk, was a cylindrical metal wastebasket. I pushed it out with my foot and looked into it. There were some scraps of paper and an envelope. I got my fingers on it and pulled it up. It was a third-class piece from a mail-order house, addressed to Mrs. Lilian W. Carmichael. I replaced it in the basket and nudged it back under the desk with my foot.

I looked at the closed bedroom door for a while. Then I heard them coming into the kitchen and went back to where I had been sitting. Donovan failed to join me, so I got up and joined him at the door. We stood with our hats in our hands, looking at Mrs. Carmichael, and she stared blankly at us from behind the hexagonal peepers. Donovan's eyes made a tour of the room and came to rest on the bedroom door.

"Anything else you'd like to tell me?" he said.

"No," she said. "I can't think of anything."

"I got to hand it to you. You had quite a lot tonight—murder in your back yard, police—and you ain't even upset."

"Lieutenant," she said, "I've lived in this city all my life. I've seen almost everything that can happen. I don't admire so-called hardened women, but I have to admit it helps over the rough spots."

While she made her speech, Donovan had moved, the way he can do it when he gets your attention on something else. Suddenly he was at that bedroom door.

"Mind if I take a look?" he said.

I watched her eyes. They blinked once and she gestured openly.

"Not at all," she said.

He twisted the knob and went in and out of sight, leaving the door partly ajar. I could see a rectangle of flowered wallpaper in the hall. A light went up. I could hear him moving around. I leaned against the wall of the vestibule that formed the front entry and looked at Mrs. Carmichael. Her blue eyes were fixed on a point just above my head.

"What is Peter Bowman in your life?" I asked.

She lowered her eyes to meet mine.

"Are you a policeman?"

"Not exactly," I said.

"I thought not."

She quit looking at me. Permanently.

Donovan came out of the bedroom hall and closed the door carefully behind him.

"I guess that's all for now," he said. "We may talk to you again."

She nodded and slipped the chain bolt.

"Good night," I said and walked away.

"Good night, Lieutenant," she said.

Donovan muttered something. I heard her door close and the rustle of the chain bolt sliding into place. On the stairs I put it up to him.

"Who was it in the bedroom?" I said. "The Mayor?"

He didn't bother with it. In the car, he directed the driver to the local station house he looked at his watch. At the station, as we entered, he looked at it again.

"Two and a half minutes," he muttered. "Mrs. Carmichael knew the Deacon was dead almost as soon as we did."

Across a wide driveway, the neon light on the old hospital building sputtered and vibrated.

CHAPTER EIGHT

At the high, old-fashioned desk of the station house, Donovan talked with a couple of plain-clothes men, giving them the description he'd got from Roberts.

"Not much," one of them said.

"It's what we've got," Donovan said.

The sergeant on the desk leaned out.

"Lieutenant, we got a call half an hour ago from Green Acres."

Donovan nodded absently.

"On the Deacon?"

"Right. It was Ward Prince himself."

"The Deacon was dead by then?"

"Uh-huh. I told him."

"Did Prince have any leads for us?"

"We were cut off. I tried to call him back but they said he wasn't there. Must have been calling from someplace else."

"All right," Donovan said.

He spent a few more minutes with the detectives. They swung away from the desk. Donovan took still another look at his watch.

"Check with me downtown in an hour," he said.

"Right, Lieutenant."

He kept looking at his watch. I could see it wasn't a new one. When he saw I was staring at him, he took one more look at the watch, then lowered his arm slowly. It came through to me, there was something he wanted me to know that he couldn't come right out with.

* * * *

We left his driver downtown and Donovan personally drove me home. During the long ride I put some things together and took others apart and when we pulled up in front of my office, I ventured to address myself to the Lieutenant.

"Cup of coffee?" I said.

"Yeah."

I brewed a potful and cut up some cheese and we sat over it.

"You going to tell me," I said, "that Deacon Roberts, with the heat he had on him, would sit around and reminisce with a total stranger and then walk into a dark alley?"

"It must have been quite a batch of money. He was way off base. He should of stayed home."

"'Home' would be Green Acres?"

"Now you're thinkin'."

I didn't know that it could be called thinking, but lights were going up in my mind as on the scoreboard of a pinball machine.

"Lloyd," I heard myself say. "Green Acres, Bowman, Lloyd, Karen, Pete—"

"What?"

"Nothing. I just went for a swim in a sea of names."

I filled his empty cup for him.

"How did he get a break like Green Acres?" I asked.

"I can guess. If he come up for parole and told the board he was afraid for his life, on account of turning in those other two, they might make a special application to Lloyd's place for him."

"All right," I said, "we don't have to fool around with it. Within five days, three people are dead of violence. They were all somewhat connected. As far as I know, there's at least one more with the same kind of connection."

He said nothing. It was mine to do something about. He had already done more than was legal in taking me on the call. I got out one of the nude snapshots and he looked at it briefly.

"Marianne McLeod," I said.

"Kind of skinny, ain't she?"

"It's an old picture. She may have filled out some."

He put the picture in his pocket.

"What happened to Anita McLeod?" I asked.

"She died a couple of years after the Deacon was sent up. They let him out to go to her funeral."

"That's pretty funny. Then they let him out to go to his own."

"Uh-huh. Well, I ain't got any more time. I got to go to work." He took out the picture and looked at it again, shaking his head sadly.

"Kid ought to eat more potatoes," he said. "So long, genius."

"So long, Commissioner."

I drank some cold coffee. It tasted as if I had made it out of somebody's ground-up gallstones. I found a piece of paper and a pencil. I wrote down the name "Carmichael, Mrs. Lilian W." I wrote "Deacon Roberts." I wrote "Lloyd" and "Karen Lloyd Bowman" and "Bowman, Pete." I wrote "Marianne McLeod."

It was about one o'clock in the morning. It would have been a dandy time to go to bed. I looked at my last remaining picture of the skinny girl. I looked at the names I had written. I went in and looked at my bed for a while. Then I went out into the lousy night.

CHAPTER NINE

There was light inside the Bowman house, but the front shades were tightly drawn. I leaned on the bell and when nothing happened, I used the brass knocker. Still nothing. I tried the knob, found the door unlocked and went on in.

She was standing a few steps up from the foot of the curving staircase with one hand on the banister and the other holding a working highball glass. She was dressed in skin-tight, peach-colored pants of a near-sheer material, with a matching blouse. Neither pants nor blouse showed any wrinkle, dip, bulge or crevice except those formed by her own personal contours. It was more a paint job than a garment. Her feet and legs were bare. Except for a purple-yellow bruise on her left cheekbone, she was the same stunning woman I had met three nights before. Also, she was stoned to the roots of her long, black hair.

I dropped my hat on a chair and took a look at the handsomely appointed room. It seemed intact, except for a small table lamp that had fallen to the floor. On the coffee table were a couple of whisky bottles, an ice hamper with some wasted cubes floating in it and one unused highball glass.

"Hi," she said. "Have a drink."

She came down the steps slowly, holding onto the banister.

"If you think you can spare it," I said.

She made an expansive gesture. Unfortunately, she used the hand with which she had been holding on and she had to grab the newel post to keep from falling. I made myself a small drink, pouring water over the whisky out of the hamper. She let go of the post and made her way unsteadily to the coffee table.

"What's your trouble?" I asked.

She frowned into the glass.

"Pete's the trouble," she said. "Remember Pete? My faithful spouse? I mean he was my faithful spouse, before he beat me up."

"I wish I could come out of one looking as good as you do."

"Anyway, he hit me. Hard."

"When?"

"Some time—is it after midnight? It was yesterday afternoon."

I tried to look sympathetic.

"And it's the first time in your life that any man raised his hand to you," I said.

"Since I was six years old."

"And it hurts."

"Yes. It hurts."

I set my glass on the coffee table, watching her. She worked her mouth, sorting out the words.

"How much does it cost to cry on your shoulder?"

"At this time of night, ten dollars an hour."

She reached out, as if to grab something, the glass slipped from her hand and she fell against me, stiff-legged.

"That's too cheap," she said. "Don't sell yourself short, Mac."

I was holding her with my right arm across her back and my left hand at her waist. Where the pants and blouse had parted, her skin was feverish. I maneuvered her to within three feet of the sofa and she gave way at the knees. I let her down easy, got my arm under her thighs and lifted her. She was not a lightweight and she gave me no help. I covered her with an afghan folded at one end of the sofa. She lay still with her eyes closed, and when I was sure she had passed well out, I went looking around.

The den was in an undisturbed condition. The FM radio was lighted and faint sputtering noises came out of it. I turned it off. There was no sign of the little package of blackmail evidence she had shown me that other night.

Upstairs, a bedroom door stood open and I went in and flipped the light switch. The room was spacious, filled with feminine fragrance. On the rumpled bed was a clutter of garments. The top item was a girdle, turned inside out. I felt the waistband and it was faintly damp. Among the garments was a set of car keys on a small chain.

On a stand near the bed was an easel, framing a photograph of a man of sixty, bald, with gentle eyes, wearing a loose-fitting white garment that suggested India. There was something familiar about his face, as if I had seen it long before. It was the only picture in the room.

A small desk was tightly locked. Under it sat a wastebasket; not the sturdy, practical tin can like Mrs. Carmichael's but a dainty receptacle in the form of a flower basket, lined and bound with a silk-like pink fabric. It contained some cigarette ashes, a few wadded papers and envelopes. There were some from Marshall Field and a couple of exclusive dress shops. Some grocery lists had been crumpled and discarded.

I spent another ten minutes on the room. There were half a dozen handbags and purses on a closet shelf, but all they contained was tissue paper.

Beyond an immaculate bathroom was Pete's room, in neat condition as before. The windows were closed and the air was faintly stale. A glamour photo of Karen stood on a high chest of drawers.

Opposite the bath, an open door led to a converted storage room, fitted out as an office with desk, typewriter stand and a filing cabinet. On the desk was one of those triangular nameplates, reading on one side, "Pete Bowman, Atty.," and on the other, "Thimk." Inasmuch as the gag motto was several years old, I gathered he had used this space in the early days for such clients as he might have picked up and later as a home study. Except for the nameplate, a blotter, a pen set and a calendar pad, the desk was clear. The top sheet on the calendar was for three days previous, Saturday. A penciled note on it read: "Marianne McL.—Rite-Spot Cafe, nights."

I leafed back through the calendar but found nothing pertinent. There were other notes, but they were out of my context. Also, when I came to think about it, they were none of my business. I held a brief struggle with my conscience and went to his files. They were built to lock, but the key was in place.

Luckily, because the name "Carmichael" came well up in the alphabet, I didn't have to snoop beyond my own tolerance. Her name was neatly typed on the index tab of a slim folder, exactly as it had appeared on her apartment door.

The principal contents of the folder consisted of a copy of a judgment of divorce, Cook County, Ill., in the case of Carmichael vs. Carmichael, brought by Mrs. Lilian W. Carmichael, granted in Superior Court, March 14, 1954. Attorney for Mrs. Carmichael was Peter Bowman. A property settlement had been approved by the court but was not detailed. Attorney's fees of $125 were to be paid by the plaintiff. Full name of the defendant was George Carmichael.

On a memo attached to the judgment were the following notations in Pete Bowman's hand:

1. L. V. Nev., $500 pd. George Carmichael, Dec. 19, 1952: C. W.
2. Fees, one dollar, pd in full, LWC, 3/14/54.

I found a pencil in the desk and made a memo of my own, copying dates and initials and noting the discrepancy between the fees granted by the court and the token fee credited by Bowman. I replaced the folder and the pencil, skimmed the rest of the file quickly and found no other names I could recognize.

I prowled the room for another few minutes. He had four or five suits hanging in the closet and a couple of pieces of luggage. There was no way for me to know whether anything was missing.

Downstairs in the den, the window shade was lowered to within three inches of the sill. I looked out and the Eldorado was parked on the drive. I went out by a French door and along the drive to the car. Its hood was warm enough to show that it had been driven recently. I went back to the garage and it was open and empty. I went back into the house.

* * * *

Mrs. Bowman was sleeping quietly where I had left her. I went to the kitchen, found a pot and brewed some coffee. There was a bottle of aspirin on a shelf and I took it back, along with the coffee and two cups.

She had begun to grow restless. Her face was mobile, wracked by shifting emotions. I was pouring the coffee when I heard a muffled cry. When I looked up, she was twisting violently. With both hands she thrust at the afghan, pushed it down, exposing a bare midriff. I rose, thinking to cover her, and she started up, blinking wildly. Her eyes found me and she quieted and settled back.

"Oh," she said. "You're over there. I thought—"

"Yes?"

She turned away.

"Nothing. I guess I was dreaming."

Pretty soon she looked at me.

"Did I say anything in my sleep?"

"No."

She put her hands to her head.

"Ooh," she said.

I sat on the edge of the sofa, helping her to the aspirin. She took it all right, leaning on her elbow, while I held the saucer and cup.

"You're a nice guy," she said. "I'm ripe to be taken advantage of, as the saying goes."

"You're also, in a way, a client."

"A client," she murmured. "How am I doing?"

"Pretty good. Once I got a call from a woman who passed out just as I was coming in the door. When she woke up, she said she had to go to the bathroom. In there, she polished off a whole bottle of sleeping pills. She damn near died on me and we hadn't said half a dozen words to each other."

"What if she had? Died, I mean."

"I'd have been in bad trouble."

Her fingers brushed at the livid laceration on her cheek.

"What led up to his hitting you?" I asked.

"Nothing. I don't know."

"You mean you were just sitting around having a drink or reading the paper and he walked over and fetched you a belt?"

She shrugged upward on the sofa and kicked the afghan away. "Maybe it was just his declaration of independence," she said.

I poured some more coffee.

"Would you like to talk about it, Mrs. Bowman?"

"Let's use first names, shall we? Mine's Karen."

"All right, Karen."

She smiled and nestled into the cushions, wriggling and stretching. Her boldly nippled breasts nudged at the soft material. The fact that I deigned to use her first name seemed a small victory for so orgasmic a satisfaction.

"How long has he really been gone?" I asked.

She looked away.

"You don't leave a girl much, do you?" she said.

"Just trying to help."

"Since Monday," she said softly. Then, more firmly, "It's happened before. He'd slam out, be gone for a couple of hours. But he always came back."

"Have you called the police?"

"No, that's out. For the usual reasons."

"All of them?"

"A good name is more to be prized than riches."

I got up and walked around, stretching my tired joints. She lay on the sofa, full-bodied in the clinging garment, watching me.

"Pete had the idea he was being led here and there by the nose?" I said.

"He didn't come right out with it."

"And that led to, say, an attack—for instance on the Lloyd Foundation, and your father?"

"We touched on it."

"And naturally you fought back."

"Like a tiger—or tigress."

"And he lost his head and laid one on you."

"And walked out."

"Uh-huh."

"Before I was through talking."

She laughed with an odd kind of delight. Her knees came up and she scratched at them.

"Was he drunk?" I asked.

"What?"

"Pete, when he walked out. I'm trying to figure his chances."

"His chances," she murmured. Her eyes found mine and held them. "You're a funny one, Mac. What do you care about Pete?" She beckoned limply and I moved nearer. I wished she would get to it. I wished she would cover herself, so it would be easier to wait it out. I wanted so I could taste it to find Pete Bowman, but the lady on the sofa was my first and so far only lead.

"You need a shave," she said sleepily. "Sit down."

She squirmed back from the edge to make room. She put one hand on my shoulder and the other on my face and rubbed against my beard.

"Mm," she said, "that's the best kind."

She took hold of my tie and pulled on it.

"Whisker me, Mac."

There were gray flecks in the brown irises of her eyes. We were so close I could only keep one of them in focus at a time.

"If it's a new game," I said, "I don't know the rules."

She lifted her head and put her cheek against mine.

"It's an old game," she said. "My father used to do it to me when I was little. I would run and he would catch me. 'I'll whisker you,' he would say. Then he would rub his face against mine, like this." She did the rubbing, not gently, holding me down with that grip on my necktie.

"Of course," she said, "akshally that's a very sekshall way for a little girl to be with her father. Does it feel sekshall to you?"

Her fingers were manipulating my ear. She wouldn't let go of my tie.

"You could have me, you know," she said. "Right now. Right here, if you want me—"

"Because I remind you of your father?"

She slipped the knot of my tie up snug against my neck.

"Not the slightest," she said.

I tried to draw back, but she held on.

"Don't you want me, Mac?"

I managed to tilt my head so I could look her in both eyes at once.

"I don't think I want to be stand-in," I said, "for whoever stood you up. Besides, the ten dollars an hour is for routine services only."

Her eyes and nostrils dilated. For about ten seconds we eyed each other silently. Then her free hand slammed against my right cheek. I felt her fingers brush my nose on the return trip and the back of her hand went at the other cheek, diamond ring and all. She had a death grip on my tie and it was affecting my wind. She got in half a dozen healthy swipes while I tried to break loose without hurting her.

I had expected it, even planned on it, but I had underestimated her physical strength. Serving both as the broken tool of her vengeance and the immediate cause of a renewed frustration, I was reaping a double harvest.

I got my feet under me and pushed with my hands against the sofa. She came up with me, hanging onto the tie and slamming me in the face. I could feel blood on it where her ring had cut in. I paid sudden slack into the tie, then jerked back and broke her grip on it. I took time to get my finger under my neckband to open the strangling noose and she rolled off the sofa, grabbing a whisky bottle as she came.

I retreated around the coffee table and her swing threw her off balance. Her knees hit the low table and she fell over it. I caught her under the arms and kept her from falling on the glasses, but she was still fighting and the only way I could hold her was to drag her across the table, wrap my arms around her waist and pull her in close. She twisted like a cat and my hands and arms were full of her, soft and yielding or bony and jutting by turns.

I was trying to talk to her, saying something like "Come on now," when the front door opened behind me. I felt cold morning air and heard quick, heavy steps, but I couldn't turn and I was afraid to let go of Karen. I remember being certain it was Pete Bowman returning and that I groped for words of explanation.

Then I was literally torn from my own grasp. My shoulder wrenched painfully and a horizontal pile driver knocked me to another part of the room. The impromptu ballet I performed en route was beyond repetition even by Red Skelton. It came to a finish against a remote wall that happened to be built stronger than my head. A couple of items of expensive furniture collapsed with me. When my eyes found the attacker, he was only an outsize blur, but I knew it couldn't be Pete Bowman, because no corporation lawyer could hit anybody that hard.

He was coming at me, following through, and I heard her yelling at him to stop. He obeyed, a little awkwardly. Gradually he became less of a blur and more of a person. Beyond him, panting and disheveled in her pink union suit, Karen Bowman, on hands and knees, was hunting for the whisky.

CHAPTER TEN

The guy stood about six-five and would weigh in at a solid two twenty. He had gray hair and about fifty years on him, but I knew him to be in fine shape. He was wearing a hat. He had a ruggedly handsome face with very alert eyes. I got the feeling that somewhere he was an important fellow, and that anywhere he would be in charge. He looked at me with the curiosity you reserve for an oddly colored beetle.

Karen had made a new drink and was holding a glass shakily. Her thick hair was snarled and the two segments of her skintight suit were twisted in opposite directions, giving her a refracted look, as if her lower half were under water and the top half out.

"Leave him alone," she said. "I asked for it."

The guy tossed his hat onto the sofa. He didn't have to look; he was at home here. Karen came over and offered me a drink. When I shook my head, she turned away. I pushed myself into a reasonable position and started to get up. The guy came and gave me a hand. I went through some surreptitious contortions and everything worked all right.

"Ward Prince," Karen said, "this is Mac—somebody—a private detective. Mr. Prince is Director of Green Acres."

He held out his hand and after examining it for brass knuckles, I shook it cautiously.

"I wish I could say it's a pleasure," I said.

He smiled. He had even, white, strong-looking teeth.

"Sorry I misinterpreted things," he said.

Karen was fingering her hair into order. She tucked her blouse into her pants and got both straightened out. I found my hat, dusted it and reshaped it.

"I'll be going," I said.

"Wait—!" Karen said.

I turned and her eyes dropped.

"Please," she said.

I stood where I was and she turned to Prince.

"Ward, would you go up and get my purse? It's in my desk—" Going obediently up the stairs, he didn't look menial. He had the dignity of a family retainer who has built his own self-esteem on the rock of unquestioning loyalty. It is the same quality that is possessed by all great soldiers, certain ecclesiastics and by most good policemen.

Karen spoke urgently to my face.

"Will you find Pete for me?"

When I didn't answer at once, she hung her head.

"I'm sorry about that—other," she said. "Can we say I was—tight?"

"You may say whatever you like," I said. "I won't be talking about it."

She was pretty game at that. She smiled.

"Please?" she said. "I'll pay—"

"Regular rates," I said.

"I'll be driving down to Green Acres this morning with Ward—Mr. Prince. You can reach me there."

There was a heavy tread on the stairs and Prince came down with a lady's purse in his big hand. Karen opened it and dug in nervously. Prince and I observed each other. I could say for him that he was a very well set up fellow. Also, apparently, something of a wizard. Her desk had been locked tight when I'd seen it, and no sign of a key.

Karen handed me a bill, negotiable for a hundred silver dollars at any Federal depository, then turned to Prince.

"Mac's going to look for Pete."

"Fine," he said. "If we can help, give us a ring. We're in the book."

"Can't you give me any kind of lead?" I asked.

"He owns a cottage at Pine Lake. It's a childhood home and like a womb to him, in a way. But I drove over there today and there was no sign of him."

"You drove the Eldorado?"

She blinked and nodded.

"Yes. I got back several hours ago."

"When Pete left, did he drive?"

"No, he just walked away. Probably took a taxi to the train, if he left town at all. He doesn't like driving, fortunately—"

"What's the number of the cottage?"

"Number 48, North Drive. It may be worth a try, but he wasn't there earlier."

"I'll do what I can," I said. "I guess you're in safe hands now."

I glanced at Prince. He smiled and nodded agreeably. I said good night and went out.

CHAPTER ELEVEN

I set my alarm for 4:00 a.m. and woke feeling like a sack of potatoes. I showered, dressed, threw some things into a bag and called my answering service to tell them I'd be gone for a while.

I got out the notes I'd made in Pete's study and dialed another number. After several rings, a man answered sleepily.

"Can you do a bank job for me?" I asked.

"For you, I guess so."

"Here are the names: Connie, or Constance Waters and/or Traven. Anita McLeod or Anita McLeod Roberts. Lilian W. Carmichael."

He was an extremely meticulous worker and I had to spell out each name and let him read it back, so it took some time. But it would pay off. His information would be as reliable as the Greenwich chronometer.

"What I want," I said, "are safe deposit boxes at Second National Bank, Branch 42 South Side—the names and dates. Okay?"

"Okay, Mac. Hurry up?"

"Always. Don't bother trying to call me. I'll keep in touch."

"Sure. Can I go back to bed now?"

"Why not?"

He hung up.

It was dawn when I got into the car and about six o'clock when I pulled up in front of the faded apartment building that housed, among others, Mrs. Lilian W. Carmichael.

She opened the door as far as the chain permitted, gave me a look through the aperture and made a sound like a cat preparing to spit. I smiled.

"If you don't let me in," I said, "I'll create a disturbance. It'll be a beaut."

The door closed. I counted to three. The chain slid free and dropped and she let me in. She was walking away as I entered. She wore a quilted housecoat of uninspired design and comfortable, floppy men's slippers. When she had looked out at me, she had been without glasses. Now, before turning, she ran her hands through her hair, rumpling it and put the glasses on.

"What do you want?" she said.

"For one thing," I said, "I want to know why you cultivate frumpiness as diligently as most women strain to avoid it."

She looked at her wrist watch.

"I'll give you five minutes to state your business," she said. "If it's legitimate, we can go on from there."

"Otherwise—?"

"I'll call the police."

She was near enough to the telephone to rest her hand on it without any strain. I think I knew right then I was licked, but the only thing riskier than launching a bluff is scuttling it ahead of the showdown.

"Go ahead," I said. "I'll wait."

She picked up the phone and started dialing. I went over and took the thing from her hand and dropped it in place.

"All right," I said, "you have nothing to fear from the police. Incidentally, neither have I."

At closer range, the anomaly between her dowdy exterior and the unmistakable feminine reality underneath was more obvious. She exuded an aura of drowsy well-being. She didn't look like a drab, sterile spinster whose total goal was to serve the bank and stay out of trouble. She looked like someone who had spent a large part of the previous night—as they used to say—"becoming a woman."

"I'm a private detective," I said, "on a legitimate inquiry. First, I'm looking for Peter Bowman. I saw his name in your list finder."

She wasn't quite looking at me now, but she wasn't cracking up either.

"Is he an attorney?" she asked.

"Yes."

"I know him. He's performed some legal services for me."

"Recently?"

"Not especially."

"Have you heard from him recently?"

"No."

"Could you tell me what he did for you in the way of legal services?"

"I could, but I won't."

She was looking at that watch again.

"Are the five minutes up?" I asked.

"Almost. Was there something else?"

"About the man who was here last night—"

"Mr. Roberts?"

"I'd like to hear the rest of that story."

"There isn't any rest of it."

She put her hand on the phone.

"Let's try this," I said. "Didn't Mr. Roberts ask you about a specific safe deposit box?"

Her eyes widened.

"At that hour? The bank was closed."

"Wasn't it about a box he wanted to look into?"

"You must be crazy."

"How much did he offer you, Mrs. Carmichael?"

"Really—" She lifted the phone and put her finger in the "WXY-9" hole. It was a slender, well-manicured finger. I put my hand on hers and she held still for it.

"I'm not on a frivolous hunt," I said. "I'm not trying to get dirt on anybody, especially you."

She glanced at our hands on the dial and I took mine away.

"Please hurry," she said. "I have only so much time in the morning—"

"But you have a lot of mornings. Others aren't so lucky. Two nights ago a man named Traven was killed in my back yard. The day before that, his wife was killed. Constance, her name was. Constance Waters Traven."

There was no change in her except a slight speed-up of her breathing. The topic alone could account for it.

"I don't see how I can help you," she said. "I'm sorry."

"Will you be sorry," I said, "when this chain of death catches up with another victim, some innocent youngster—?"

She drew herself up very straight.

"Don't try to frighten me," she said. "Your time is more than up. Please go."

I tried to stare her down, but it was like trying to outface the Mona Lisa. She followed me to the door without crowding.

"There's one more question," I said, "personal."

"What?"

"How long did you and George Carmichael live together as man and wife?"

"Get out," she said.

"Five hundred dollars should have been good for at least one night."

Now, if ever, I thought, those cool blue eyes would register an emotion, would snap or flash, distort, widen or narrow.

I was wrong. I looked straight into them and it was like looking at the façade of a skyscraper. At night. After the lights have been turned out and the people have all gone home.

CHAPTER TWELVE

Pine Lake in the early morning was a placid, blue-green pond a mile long and three quarters of a mile across at the widest point. The Green Acres farm bordered a third of its length off to my left.

Steel City had Green Acres the way Chicago has stockyards and New York the Statue of Liberty. I had driven past its rolling, fertile fields, had seen from a distance the tightly fenced cluster of trees and buildings that formed its nucleus, the old Lloyd estate. I had never been on the grounds.

I knew about it the way you know about the government or the Carnegie Endowment or the United Nations. I knew it was operated by the Lloyd Foundation as a rehabilitation center for parolees and probationers; that it was the outgrowth of a philanthropy started on a small scale by Calvin Lloyd's long deceased wife. I knew its reputation—and his—was impeccable among local judges, who would frequently substitute probation for a jail term, if the convictee would agree to a stint at Green Acres. I knew it had a long waiting list.

Also I knew the rough outline of the legend of Calvin Lloyd, who had achieved local sainthood in his lifetime. I had never met him, nor, until a few hours earlier, any of his staff, which was headed by the ex-policeman, Ward Prince. He was barely short of legendary himself, with a reputation for decisiveness, scrupulous dealing and absolute loyalty. Around Steel City it was said that if the President of the United States were to ask Ward Prince to be the Chief Justice of the Supreme Court, he would say, "I'll have to ask Mr. Lloyd."

* * * *

I turned right on a road that skirted the lake northward. Near the turn were a cluster of cheap, shack-like cottages, a public picnic area, a few rowboats upside down on the shore. The road was in preseason condition—very bad.

Beyond the public facilities, I drove among trees. The lots were bigger, the cottages secluded. I saw little recent construction. Most of the places were heavily shuttered and I saw none that was currently occupied. The season wouldn't open for another month.

The farther north I went, the more spacious were the sites and buildings. Some had garages. At one, obviously not occupied, the garage door stood open.

Number 48 North Drive was an English cottage with low-hanging eaves and ivy. A driveway curved in to an arched, oak door, then continued back to the road. There was no garage. The windows were shuttered with solid frames nailed on from the outside.

There was no doorbell. When I knocked, the sound was fragile, without echo. I followed a cinder path to the lake side of the cottage. A screened porch ran the width of the building, overlooking the water. There was a small dock. A porch door opened on a short flight of steps to the ground level. There were no shutters on the porch screens, but all the windows on the inner wall were covered, except for a kitchen door leading from the porch into the cottage. There had been a shutter here too, but it had been removed and was leaning against the wall beside the door. A green shade on the window was drawn on the inside. The door was locked. I felt along the top of the jamb and picked up a handful of dust. I looked down at the straw mat on which I stood, stepped off it and rolled back the edge. There was the key.

Despite the shutters and the appearance of long abandonment, the air inside was fresh. I flipped a light switch in the kitchen. The stove and refrigerator were very old, but clean. In the refrigerator were a carton half full of milk and four eggs. There was a small pile of unwashed dishes in the sink and on a piece of waxed paper was a mound of used coffee grounds.

The living room was filled with the odds and ends of furniture that people allot to a summer cottage. Nothing matched anything else, but it was all comfortable. There was a flat couch along one wall with an army blanket folded at the foot. Over a corner fireplace was an empty mahogany gun mount. On the mantel stood a pipe rack with half a dozen pipes in it.

A curtained arch led to an adjoining room opposite the couch. The curtains were gray monk's cloth, faintly ragged at the bottom. On one of them was pinned a large red heart cut out of paper, such as a child might make at school. There was nothing else unusual about them except that protruding between them, aimed in my direction, was a six-inch length of the barrel of the rifle that ought to have been in the mantel mount.

I froze awkwardly, my feet crooked, with one hand partly raised and the hair pushing at my hat in back. I had no famous last thoughts. I had no thoughts at all. The worst thing about it was the eternal silence. I felt I had to break it, but when I said the words, they made no sound. I ran my tongue over my lips and tried again. They squeaked, but they came out.

"I have no gun. I mean no harm."

Nothing brilliant about it, but it was the best I had. The blue-black muzzle described an eccentric arc, then retraced it like a runaway eye and came to rest. It was so quiet now I could hear us breathing; mine alternately suppressed and explosive; the other's more regular, but hoarse and short. A causeless breeze ruffled one of the curtains and the paper heart rustled.

"How about—" I said—"we talk it over?"

Another eternity dragged by. The gun muzzle fanned the air and leveled and the barrel started into the room. The curtains billowed outward, the polished wooden grip pushed through and there was a slim hand on it and another on the barrel itself. Then the stock and two thin, freckled arms. The curtains didn't have to spread much to let the rest of her into the room. I waited, watching her, in stocking feet, dressed in a stained blue cotton uniform such as a waitress would wear, with thin arms and legs and her shoulders hunched with the gun burden, and the light-colored disheveled hair—and everywhere, except around her timeless eyes, she was a child. Against the background of those same curtains, the same girl had looked at me out of a photograph, but with another kind of look.

She held the gun clumsily with her left hand too far out on the barrel. It was heavy for her. The corners of her mouth were drawn down and the suspicion and fear in her ancient eyes were as much a part of her as the color of her hair and the shape of her bones. But her finger would have to travel three inches to get at the trigger and I shifted my position to stand more easily. My smile cracked my face like heat cracking varnish.

"Marianne McLeod, isn't it?" I said.

Her mouth twitched. Her eyes didn't change.

"Who are you?"

"You can call me Mac."

"I don't know you. How'd you know me?"

She stood flat on her left foot and scratched her calf with her right instep.

"You a cop?" she said.

"No."

Her eyes wandered over the room, haunting it. When they got back on me, they wanted me to do something, to take charge. But they wanted to be safe behind the gun too.

"I'm looking for Peter Bowman," I said.

"You from Chicago?"

"That's right."

"I was there once."

I shrugged to ease the pressure of my neckband.

"Well, if Pete were here," I said, "he'd have heard us by now. I'll be going."

I turned away and there was a light thud. I looked around and she had lowered the stock of the rifle to the floor and was holding it by the barrel loosely, running one finger idly around the rim of the muzzle.

"He's in there," she said.

I glanced at the quiescent curtains. She was still fooling with the rifle muzzle.

"Don't get a finger stuck in there," I said, "we might have to shoot it out."

She stopped fingering it and held it with the barrel resting against her thigh. I started toward the arch, pausing beside her.

"Must be heavy," I said.

I slid my hand around the barrel below hers and she let go of it. I lifted it clear of the floor and carried it on through the arch into a good-sized bedroom. There was a matching three-piece set, including a bureau, a dressing table and a bed. Pete Bowman, fully dressed, was on the bed.

He would have been sitting or standing at the foot of it and he would have died in the process of falling back onto the bed, from the combined impact of the bullet at close range and the sudden, total, irrevocable loss of nervous initiative. So that about the best you could say for it was that it had been clean, instantaneous and painless. It was not at all a bad way to go, but it was too bad that the going had been necessary at his age and with what, I presumed, he had to live for. There I could have been wrong.

His feet hung clear of the floor by an inch or two. Under the heel of his right shoe was a piece of oil-stained flannel. On a paper towel near the off leg of the bedstead was a small can of high-grade machine oil. So it could have been that he had been cleaning the rifle and if he had been a little high or very tired or upset about something, and careless…

All things were possible.

CHAPTER THIRTEEN

Marianne stood on the outer edges of her little feet, working her toes spasmodically. A pair of dirty white sandals was on the floor near the bed.

I lifted the gun and sighted along the barrel, opened it and examined the chamber. It appeared to have been fired either since the cleaning or before there had been time to complete it. I moved reluctantly to the bed and put the back of my hand against Pete's outflung wrist. It was cold, not rigid. At a rough guess, it had happened before midnight and after the previous sundown.

I looked at Marianne and she twisted her toes.

"How long have you been here?" I asked.

"About a half hour," she said.

"He was like this when you came?"

"Yeah."

"How did you get in?"

She pulled a key from her uniform pocket.

"He gave it to me at the place."

"What place?"

"Where I work. A restaurant."

"When did he give it to you?"

"Last night. How come you ask so many questions if you're not a cop?"

"I'm a private cop. I've been looking for Pete Bowman. By a strange coincidence, I was looking for you too."

"Why me?"

It just didn't seem like the time to tell her, if she didn't know, that I had watched her stepfather die less than twelve hours earlier.

"Where was the gun when you came in?" I asked.

"Right there."

She pointed to the floor at the foot of the bed. I got out my handkerchief and wiped barrel, stock and rest thoroughly. Holding it with my handkerchief, I laid it down, watching her for directions. "How was it?" I asked.

"What do you mean? It was just laying there."

"Which way did it point? Like this?"

"No," she said, "the other way. Turn it over."

It was more likely to have been that way if it had fallen from his hand.

"Push it back a little," she said.

She stood with her hands on her hips and her funny little freckled face tilted.

"That's where it was," she said.

"And you picked it up when you heard me come in?"

"Yeah. I didn't know who it was—"

"Maybe you'd like to put on your shoes."

She went to where they were and stepped into them, glancing at Pete.

"He was a nice guy," she said. "It sure surprised me to come in and find him like that."

"Why did he ask you to come out here?"

"I don't know. I've been here before, a long time ago."

"Oh?"

"With Connie. Connie Traven. A friend of mine. She's dead. Her lousy husband killed her."

"I read about it."

"She was the best friend I ever had."

"Why did Pete give you the key?"

"He said in case he wasn't here, so I could get in."

She stamped her feet hard to settle her shoes.

"You have anything else here besides the shoes?"

"No. I came right from work."

There was a telephone on a bedside table. I put it to my ear and the line was dead. I leaned over the man on the bed, avoiding his eyes, and started through his pockets.

"He didn't have any money on him," she said. "I already looked." I glanced at her and she looked away.

"Well," she said, "what would he care now?"

"I guess he wouldn't care."

"That's what you're looking for, isn't it?"

"No."

His wallet was in his jacket pocket. It contained a driver's license, a couple of credit cards, a snapshot of his wife, Karen, in a bathing suit, a few restaurant tab receipts and no money. I put everything back where I had found it and replaced the wallet. In his shirt pocket was a package of cigarettes and a match folder with a picture of a bird on it in color.

I had to work slowly on his pants pockets because it was hard to get into them without disarranging him. Marianne watched me with a childish fascination, her lips parted, her breath short and irregular. I had my hand in his left pocket.

"You overlooked something," I said. "A nickel."

She stuck her nose in the air and turned away. I raised him enough to get at his hip pockets. He was heavy with his feet hanging over the edge. One pocket was flat, the other contained a clean handkerchief. The outside pockets of his jacket yielded a couple of empty match folders and a bar tab with the corner nipped off. There was no business name on it, but on the plain side was a scrawled message in pencil: "Vit stat. Mr. Crowley." I put it in my pocket.

On the telephone stand and the bureau there was the normal small, personal clutter. Marianne spoke up in a thin, piping voice. "If we're going to hang around, can I take my shoes off?"

"We won't be long," I said. "Did you touch anything else while you were here?"

"No"

"Nothing? Did you use the bathroom?"

"That's a pretty personal question."

"Excuse me."

I went through a dressing alcove with a closet and into a small bathroom. There was no particular muss. I flushed the toilet for luck and wiped off the handle and the handles of the taps in the basin. There was a turkish towel on an aluminum rack and I wiped the rack with the towel and left it hanging.

In a wastebasket under the lavatory were some scraps of paper. I found two halves of a letter addressed to Mr. Peter Bowman at a Steel City P. O box. The letterhead read: Abbott Farrell, C. P. A., at a Steel City address. The letter was dated two days previously. I folded the two halves and put them in my pocket, without taking time to read them. There was no envelope, but he could have thrown that away downtown.

When I got back to the bedroom, Marianne was busily wiping off the knobs of the bureau drawers with a piece of tissue. She tossed her head defiantly.

"I was just looking for a towel," she said. "Anyway, they're my fingerprints; what's it to you?"

"I don't know," I said.

She stuck the tissue in her pocket.

"Where's that key he gave you?" I asked.

She produced it hesitantly.

"If it should be found on you," I said, "you'd be in trouble. All right if I take care of it?"

"I guess so."

I took it, not without a sudden qualm. I had been making very free with the entire scene and was about to make still freer. But people had been dying like flies and Marianne had a good chance of being next in line, and the police are specialists in the apprehension of crime, not in its prevention.

I went into the living room and she stalked me.

"What're you going to do?" she said.

"I'm going to give you a ride home."

"I don't know—"

"Would you rather stay and talk to the cops?"

She stood there with her chin out.

"I'll have to call them."

"What'll you tell them?"

I shrugged. She would have to worry some. Everybody has to worry. It's a duty.

"How did you get out here?" I asked.

"Charlie brought me in a taxi. Pete gave me the money for it."

"But Charlie didn't wait for you?"

"I told him not to wait."

Charlie would remember the fare. Seven-thirty in the morning and the lonely drive around the lonely lake and the Bowman cottage.

"You sure you had nothing else with you?" I said. "No coat, sweater, anything like that?"

"I left my sweater in the taxi. I forgot it."

"Oh. Well, Charlie will keep it for you."

"Sure."

"My car's out front. Go ahead and get in it. I'll be right with you.

She hesitated, then, shrugging in that world-weary way, she turned and trudged outside. I wiped off both knobs of the door and the edge for a foot or so above and below the knobs and up and down the door jamb. I pushed it to, made sure it was locked and went out on the screened porch. I locked the kitchen door and replaced the key under the mat. I went out by the screen door and down the steps and stopped, watching the lake.

CHAPTER FOURTEEN

An aluminum rowboat was skimming the quiet surface, heading for the Bowman dock. The man in it, stripped to the waist, rowed expertly, with a steady, controlled rhythm. He was bald and the top of his head shone bright in the sun.

He looked around to check his bearing, backwatered, then shipped his oars and glided smoothly alongside the dock. I walked through a grove of elm trees. The ground was spongy underfoot. I walked out onto the planking and squatted, looking at him in the boat.

He was maybe sixty-five and nut-brown all over. He wore a pair of khaki shorts and straw sandals. He was in as good a shape for his age as I had ever seen. He had bright blue eyes that probed shrewdly at mine.

"You have business here?" he said.

"I may have."

"I saw you coming out of the cottage. It belongs to my son-in-law and his wife—"

"Karen and Pete Bowman," I said.

"Then you know them."

"In Chicago." I held out my hand, gave him my name and profession. The brown skin wrinkled at the corners of his eyes.

"Nothing wrong, I hope," he said.

I spread my hands.

"You would be Mr. Lloyd."

We shook hands. There was something about him over and above his legend. I could feel it. I could know, just meeting this man, that I was all right with him until proven otherwise.

"Pete's been away from home for a day," I said. "We were looking into it."

"Karen thought he might have come here?"

"That was a possibility."

"But he wasn't here?"

"No. He wasn't here."

If I was the first in twenty years to pull wool over his eyes, I had no feeling of accomplishment. But because of the young woman in my car, I felt at the same time that I had no alternative.

I looked across the lake toward his landing and the newly turned, rolling fields of Green Acres. A couple of tractors crawled back and forth. A man walked out onto a dock, stood a moment, then turned and went away. It would be close to a mile at this angle: a long way to see a man coming out of a tree-screened cottage, even with the morning sun on your shoulder.

His shrewd eyes followed my gaze and the skin wrinkled high on his face as he shook his head.

"No, I didn't see you from over there," he said. "This is my morning constitutional. I find rowing a congenial exercise, inexpensive and convenient." He went a little shy. "I rowed on the Princeton crew, a good many years ago."

"I'm sure you could hold your own with the best they ever had," I said.

I straightened to my feet. The green water around the idly bobbing boat was a clear mirror.

"I have to be going," I said.

"I hope you'll visit us," he said. "You're always welcome at Green Acres."

I nodded gravely. We waited through two watch ticks, each for the other to take leave.

"When you find Pete," he said, "you might ask him to get in touch with me, if he's inclined. I'm very fond of Peter."

I nodded, backing away.

"Nice to have met you, Mr. Lloyd."

"Good day," he said.

He pushed strongly against the dock with one hand, brought his oar into play and headed into the sun. As I found solid ground with my feet, he was rowing with long, sure strokes toward home.

* * * *

There was no place to park in front of the top-heavy frame building she called home. A battered sign read: "rooms." An old man in shirt sleeves sat in a porch swing. There were some patches of dirty brown grass in the front yard.

I pulled into the curb. She had made the ten-mile trip with her mouth shut and her eyes open. Getting next to her was going to be like opening a can with your teeth.

"What were you in for?" I asked.

Sitting hard by the door, ready to leap and run for cover, she fingered the handle nervously.

"Where do you get off with a question like that if you're not a cop? I don't have to talk to you."

"It would be worth money to me," I said.

"What for—just to talk?"

"Yes. Talk about you, about Pete Bowman—and Connie Traven and Deacon Roberts. About your mother, Anita McLeod."

Her gray-green eyes squinted at me.

"They're all dead. What's the point?"

"Doesn't it give you a funny feeling to realize they're all dead—and that three of them died within the last week?"

"What're you, trying to scare me?"

"I'm trying to help you. If you went out there to the cottage and Pete tried to start something and you grabbed that gun and shot him—"

"I didn't!"

"Will you stay here till I come back!"

"Where would I go?"

Her hand deviled the door latch.

"What about the cops?" she said. "What am I supposed to say?"

"They won't get around to you before I get back."

"But what if they do?"

"Tell them Pete asked you to go to the cottage. You went in a taxi. The taxi left and you couldn't get into the cottage. Nobody answered the door. Pretty soon I came along and gave you a ride back to town."

"Yeah, but who are you?"

"A private eye from Chicago. They'll know me. But I'll be back before they show up."

"You better," she said. "Because you're right, I'm on parole. They keep coming around."

She got out and stood looking in through the open window. "You'll be back, for sure?" she said.

"For sure."

It meant something to her.

"How did you know about the Deacon?" I said. "It only happened last night."

"A guy told me." Her fingers worked along the window ledge like a cook's trimming pie crust. "Some fellow hangs around. Nicky."

"Nicky's a special friend of yours?"

"He hangs around."

"All right, Marianne, you take it easy. We'll talk later."

She couldn't seem to let go of the car.

"The Deacon was nuts," she said. "He was safe out there at Green Acres. He never should have left."

"You know about Green Acres?"

Her mouth twisted.

"I ought to," she said. "I was born there."

On this note of high triumph, she turned and stalked off toward the old rooming house. She had scored one on me. She had status.

CHAPTER FIFTEEN

The man who came out of the gatekeeper's lodge at Green Acres was neither friendly nor hostile. His blue serge suit was an expensively perfect fit. He had the quiet alertness of the trained watchdog and he would hire for a lot more money than Donovan could ever expect to draw in the civil service. I showed him my ID card and he waved me on toward an electronically operated gate, set in a high steel wire fence surrounding the original Lloyd home.

The gate's timing was precise. It opened as I approached and I had just cleared it, at twenty mph, when it began the return trip. The drive wound up to an imposing colonial building with a parking area in front. The deep porch was five steps up from the ground. A brass plate in the top step read: *"Green Acres—Admin. Bldg."* As I climbed over it, a glass-paneled door opened and the gatekeeper's twin brother escorted me personally into a spacious foyer.

Facing the main entrance was a full-length portrait of a woman in formal dress. It was a good portrait and the dress dated it at around 1930. She was a striking woman, tall, slender, bearing some resemblance to Karen Bowman, who was standing now below the portrait, in low-voiced conversation with Ward Prince. She had changed to a more and less fitting costume than she had worn earlier in the morning. She nodded tiredly. The dark pouches under her eyes were scar-like in her pale face.

Prince greeted me with a handshake and we passed the time of day. I couldn't quite get around to the message. It was Karen who sensed that all was not well. She left Prince and came to me slowly, her brown eyes searching.

"It's about Pete," she said. "You found him?"

"I'm sorry," I said. "At the cottage. He's dead."

Her eyes closed and she swayed. Prince put an arm around her in a protective way.

"How—?" she said. "What happened?"

"I'm not sure. There was a gun. He'd been shot."

She pried her eyes open, looked at each of us in turn and, pushing at her hair, turned away.

"I'll be in my apartment," she said.

We watched her cross the foyer and go out by a side exit. Prince's face was tight.

"In here," he said.

I followed him into a plain but spacious office. It had a large desk and half a dozen matching chairs. There was a single picture on the wall, an English hunting scene. Prince went to his desk and I sat on one of the chairs.

"You are the one who found him?" he said.

I nodded.

"When?"

I told him.

"Have you reported it to anyone else?"

"Only to you and Mrs. Bowman."

"Not the police?"

"I wasn't working for the police."

He knuckled the table for about three seconds. Then he reached for his phone and dialed three numbers. I heard an answering click.

"Ward Prince," he said. "I'd like Chief Harrison."

Naturally, from here you would go to the top.

"Chief," he said, "we have a violent death to report. At Pine Lake. Number forty-eight North Drive. We'll give you more details when you want them."

He listened a moment.

"No publicity if you can possibly avoid it," he said. "Thank you." He hung up.

There must have been something in my face because after a moment he said, "It's county, but the Sheriff is understaffed and the city police handle the Pine Lake area. Sheriff's happy to be shut of it."

Pretty soon he said, "You must have some idea of what it takes to stay on top of an operation like this. One thing is a working relationship with the Steel City authorities based on complete mutual trust."

"I understand," I said, "but I'm not an institution."

He wasn't quite satisfied.

"Naturally," I said, "I'll confirm that I discovered Pete."

He relaxed some.

"Actually, I'm glad you came to us first—Pete's being a member of the family. Want to fill me in?"

I told him everything just as it happened, but leaving out all reference to Marianne and my fooling around with the gun and fingerprints. He was an attentive audience.

"Is that it?" he said when I stopped.

"Just about. As I was leaving, by way of the screened porch, Mr. Lloyd rowed up to the dock and we had a few words together."

His alert eyes fixed.

"Did you tell Mr. Lloyd what you'd found?"

"No. I hadn't told Mrs. Bowman yet."

"I can see your motive, but for future reference, it is always best to tell Mr. Lloyd anything you think might be of interest to him."

"Now that I understand," I said.

"Why did you go through his pockets?"

"To find out whether they contained any useful information. I am a very ripe market for information at this time."

"On Mrs. Bowman's behalf?"

I shrugged and he let it go.

"You think he was shot accidentally?" he asked.

"There was the stuff you would use to clean the gun," I said. "I don't see what other conclusion they can come to, unless they find evidence that someone had been with him."

"You found no such evidence?"

"No," I said.

He put his hands flat on the desk. They were strong-looking, immaculate, without scar or blemish.

"I'd like to ask you a question," he said.

"I'll deal, question for question."

"If I can."

"That's fair."

"What happened between you and Sergeant Downs over that Traven affair?"

"Nothing much. The Sergeant shot Traven in the back and I got sick to my stomach."

"Is that what got Pete so worked up?"

"Well, the fact that Traven was his friend and that he was shot down without a trial—"

"So he decided to clear Traven's name?"

"That's what he said."

"That's all he wanted? Just to clear Traven?"

"That's all I know of."

He seemed to think it over.

"My turn?" I asked.

"Go ahead."

"What was Deacon Roberts going for?"

"I wish I knew. He was a fool to get caught."

"He must have had a strong motive."

"Maybe."

"You've discussed it with Lieutenant Donovan?"

He blinked a couple of times.

"Matter of fact, yes," he said. "This morning."

I found myself looking at my watch, though I knew very well what time it was.

"And got out to Mrs. Bowman's just in time to save her from a fate worse than death."

His smile was a little tight.

"Sorry about that," he said.

It had been unnecessary, but maybe not useless. It put us on more equitable terms.

"Could I see Mrs. Bowman for a minute?" I asked. "I'd like to extend my sympathy."

"I'll call her."

He picked up the phone and I heard him talking to her. No sooner had he hung up than it rang and while he took the call, I wandered out to the foyer. Prince joined me after two or three minutes. I was looking at the portrait of the handsome woman.

"Mrs. Lloyd?" I said.

Prince looked up as if at a shrine.

"A great woman," he said. "You'd never forget her."

"I didn't realize you'd been here that long."

He emitted pride like static.

"I came out from the East," he said, "in 1936, on a routine mission, to interview an ex-convict. This was two years before she died. I stayed a few days, but it didn't take that long really. Two hours with Mrs. Lloyd and I was completely under her spell. When Mr. Lloyd established the Foundation and needed a man to head it up, I jumped at the chance."

I could believe him. He'd been in his twenties then.

* * * *

Karen was lying on a Victorian chaise longue, a blanket drawn up to her waist. The apartment had been converted from an old carriage house and the lower floor was given over to garage space. There was a view of the lake some distance off across the fields.

"Would he have suffered much?" she asked.

"Not at all."

She pushed the blanket away and got up and we stood side by side, looking out over the lake.

"In a way it's fitting it should have happened at the cottage," she said, "the cradle of our romance."

She laughed harshly and stopped suddenly.

"I'm listening," I said.

"Script by Fitzgerald, music by Cole Porter," she said. "I was the girl next door, until Pete's father lost his money and they moved out to the lake. His father died there. Drowned himself. I didn't see Pete for years—maybe off and on. There was the Korean War; Pete was in it.

"We ran into each other one night at a cocktail party, at the country club, of course. It was a dull party and we sneaked out. We drove out to the cottage. We built a fire and lay around on the rug and talked old times and deep philosophy. We got pretty high. That's part of the rules—like ducking out of the country club, like sitting on the floor and having to go through the philosophy bit before getting down to basic matters. Another rule is that sometime during the evening, you have to go for a swim."

I looked at her and she nodded solemnly.

"We did. Damn near froze to death."

I happened to have a clean handkerchief.

"My God, shut me off, Mac," she said.

"Running water is the cleanest," I said.

"Sure it is." She worked at her eyes. "We had some dates after that. Pete was in his last year of law school and he was broke."

She returned the handkerchief.

"I don't have to tell you, do I? It was a setup. It was time to get married. I was a girl who had to be in charge. Pete was asking for it."

I turned from the window and she caught at my sleeve.

"There's my father!"

It was the tone you reserve for exclaiming at a sunrise. There was a small stone cottage fifty yards away toward the lake. Calvin Lloyd, in his shorts, was doing yoga exercises in the yard, sitting with arms and legs folded.

"He lives there alone," she said. "Nobody is allowed in there, not even me. He's a very great man."

"I believe it."

"He wasn't always. Before, he was—like Pete, a playboy. Fun like Pete, but just a playboy. Then he changed. It was like a conversion. Of course nobody would believe it for a long time. When he was trying to get Green Acres started on a big scale, everybody fought him—police, the courts, newspapers—they didn't trust him. No character, they said. But thanks to Ward Prince, we made it."

"Prince did most of it?"

"Ward Prince," she said, "is terrific, fabulous. But it could never have got where it did without my father. In the public eye, where it counts, Green Acres is Calvin Lloyd."

Mr. Lloyd sat like a Buddha on the ground in front of his stone hut. I believed what his daughter had told me. But I remembered how he had told me, with shy pride, that he had once rowed on the Princeton crew.

Karen saw me to the door. I was looking at the bruise on her cheek. Her eyes held for a minute, then wandered.

"It wasn't Pete who struck me," she said. "It was—some man who came to see him."

"A client of Pete's?"

"No. He was uncouth, out of the gutter. It was a little while before you came. I guess it's really what made me get so—drunk."

"What did this fellow want?"

"He wouldn't say. I told him Pete wasn't home and he got that look in his eye. He said something like, 'Honey, I guess you'll do,' then, without any preliminaries, he made a direct, physical pass. When I resisted, he hit me."

"And gave up?"

"Yes—all at once. I don't know why, except he was very young. And he couldn't know but what there might be someone else in the house."

"What did he look like?"

"Short, stocky, swarthy complexion, flashy clothes—" I nodded gravely.

"Anything else? Did he mention his name?"

"Not that I—wait—yes! When I opened the door he said, 'Tell Pete that so-and-so wants to see him.' It was—Dicky—Ricky—something—"

"Like Nicky?"

"Yes. It could have been. Nicky."

I got the door open and she smiled a little.

"I'm sorry I couldn't find Pete sooner," I said. "I'll be at the Prescott Hotel if you need me."

I needn't have worried about that, I thought, going down the steps. The Lloyds are the self-sufficient type, give or take an occasional light belt from a mysterious stranger named Nicky.

* * * *

Leaving the estate, I got through the big gate all right, but at the gate-keeper's lodge, the ex-secret service man was waiting with his hand up. I stopped. Ward Prince came out of the lodge and looked in at me.

"I just heard," he said, "about a complication in Pete's case."

"Oh?" I said.

"Some cab driver downtown says he took a young woman out to the cottage early this morning—a Marianne McLeod."

I looked at my watch and swore mentally at Donovan. He had me doing it. Every time anyone spoke to me lately, I looked at my watch.

"I'm at a disadvantage," I said. "I haven't seen this cab driver."

"You didn't see anyone else while you were there?"

"I saw Mr. Lloyd."

"But nobody else?"

"Unless she was hiding in a drainpipe—" He looked at me for a while and finally he pushed back from the car and nodded goodbye.

"All right, Mac," he said. "Let's keep in touch."

He waved me on and I rolled down the winding road to the highway, staying well within the posted speed limit. On the main road, however, heading for town, I was under a different jurisdiction. With it, since I helped to support it, I could take my chances.

CHAPTER SIXTEEN

Climbing the warped stairs of the faded rooming house, time chased me like a fresh runner in an old race. I brushed past an aged fellow in a bathrobe, heard him muttering about people in a hurry.

At the back of the third floor hall, her name had been written in pencil on a piece of paper torn from an envelope and fixed on the door with Scotch tape. I knocked and nothing happened. I put my ear to the panel and knocked some more.

"Who is it?" she said sleepily.

I told her. I heard bedsprings, a small thudding of bare feet.

"Wait till I say come in," she said.

I waited with my hand full of doorknob.

"Come in!"

She was settling down in a brass bed, covered to the shoulders with a sheet and one cotton blanket.

"I sleep raw," she said. "I didn't know you'd be back so soon."

There were the bed and a narrow dresser, topped by an oval mirror in a dark frame. The mirror was cracked. There were a straight chair and an alcove with built-in shelves and a curtain strung on a wire. A couple of cotton dresses hung from a hook on the door. The dresser top was cluttered with paper, cosmetics and a few coins. In an ornate gilt frame was an enlarged color photo of a vivid blonde, inscribed in a bold, free hand, "To Marianne with love—Connie." Her eyes were deep blue, set back under a jutting brow. There was something so startlingly familiar about her that I had to force myself to look away. Marianne's eyes were blinking rapidly.

"That's Connie. She was my best friend," she said.

I sat down on the chair and she watched me steadily, her head propped on a soiled pillow.

"Who is this Nicky you mentioned?" I asked.

"Nicky? He's just around—I told you—"

"What does he do for a living?"

"I don't know. Different things. He plays the horses. He gives me tips."

"Does he do anything else?"

"Sure. He was doing some time for a while. Only he did it at Green Acres. They said he stole a car."

"They were probably just against him."

"Is Nicky what you wanted to talk about?"

"Not entirely."

The smells and the soiled clothing and the dust and the hard, calculating look in her eyes were getting under my skin.

"You're in some trouble, you know," I said.

"I didn't do anything!"

"Maybe not. But you're the only one who knows it and you're on parole."

She started up, grabbing at the sheet.

"Did you tell the cops I was—you dirty—"

"No. But sooner or later it will get around that Pete Bowman was shot and Charlie will remember."

"Listen, you, I didn't shoot him."

"All right."

Something had finally got to her. She was scared and it showed. "Look, I can't get mixed up in it. That parole officer—if I step out of line for one minute—"

"Take it easy. I'll help you. I need help too. And I'll pay."

"What kind of help?"

"Research. Nothing strenuous. You'll move out of here for a few days. I'll get a place for you."

"I don't know about any research. You mean reading books, like that?"

"Very light work. How much do you make now?"

"With tips—forty-five, fifty a week."

"I'll pay you fifteen dollars a day."

"I don't know—what about my job?"

"What happens if you get sick?"

"I call one of the day girls and she works for me. Then I split my tips with her the next week."

"So now you're sick. A few days. You have to go to the hospital."

"Hospital! What for?"

"I don't know! To have your tonsils out. What's the difference?"

"I don't know. I never saw you before—"

"Have I given you any trouble?"

"Boy, you better not."

She sank back, chewing at her lip.

"All right," she said. "But no funny stuff."

"No funny stuff, whatever that is."

"You know what I mean. Men think a girl that's done some time will do anything."

"Relax. I'll wait outside while you dress. Better not wear the uniform, huh?"

"I can at least dress myself. Go on out."

In the hall I leaned against the door, waiting. The old house creaked and rumbled under me. When she came out, she wore a flared print skirt and a sweater, the sandals and white ankle socks. She had two bright dabs of rouge on her cheeks and an orange-red mouth. She had the portrait of Connie, too, hugged tight against her breast.

"Won't you want a change or two?" I said.

She turned back and I caught her arm.

"Let it go," I said. "We can pick up something."

I reached quickly for the door. A half-set, rough-edged screw on the metal lock plate gouged at my thumb. I slammed the door and put the thumb to my mouth. When I held it down to look at it, Marianne flattened against the wall. Two white rings showed around the spots of rouge.

"Wrap it up," she said hoarsely. "I can't stand that stuff."

I got out the handkerchief Karen had cried in.

"That sounds funny," I said, "the way you rolled that corpse for loose change."

"That was different," she said. "He was dead."

"Next time, I'll manage to die."

She kept quiet.

* * * *

At the downtown bus terminal, I pulled into the parking lot. When I tried to help her out, she hung back.

"You didn't say we were going on a bus."

"We're not going on a bus," I said.

She came along.

"The minute I get out of line," I said, "you have my permission to scream."

"Don't think I won't."

"Scream good and loud. Don't spare the tonsils."

I held the door for her and, in passing, she said, "I'm having my tonsils out, remember?"

We headed for the lunch counter.

"So you are," I said. "And you're some girl. I don't know if I can keep up with you."

"Don't strain yourself," she said.

I'll bet you were a ball at the candy store, I thought.

At the counter, she ordered a hot dog and a bottle of a nationally advertised, sweet, dark-colored, carbonated beverage. "Nothing else?" I said. "Cole slaw, glass of milk?"

"Huh-huh. I mostly like hot dogs."

When the waitress brought the first hot dog, Marianne looked at her, very haughty, and said, "Bring me some mustard."

The waitress glanced at me.

"Please," I said.

She brought the mustard.

"Thank you," I said.

Marianne dug in, chewing thoughtfully.

"You're real polite, huh?" she said.

"Doesn't hurt anything."

"I wish all my customers were like you."

"The girls work hard for their money."

"Not any harder than I do."

"All right," I said.

I excused myself and crossed the concourse to the telephone booths. After some brief research, I got on the line with a pleasant-voiced woman who managed a transient apartment building in the downtown area.

"Something for my daughter and myself for a few days," I said.

"We don't have any two-bedroom—"

"Is there a couch in the living room?"

"Yes."

"That will be fine. We're at the bus station. It'll be about half an hour."

I opened the door so she could get the sound effect of a bus station. She said she'd have it ready.

Back at the counter a young guy was sitting on the stool next to Marianne. I got into my own place and picked up my cold hamburger.

"Look who's here," she said. "Nicky."

"Hello, Nicky," I said.

"Hi," he said.

CHAPTER SEVENTEEN

His complexion wasn't too swarthy. He was of medium size, skinny, not stocky. He had very white teeth. His suit was sharply cut, inexpensive but clean and stiffly pressed. His mouth twitched.

"I didn't catch the last name," I said.

"Royal. Nick Royal."

"This is Mac," Marianne said. "Mac, say hello to Nicky."

"I did," I said.

He nodded jerkily at Marianne.

"Some kid," he said. "She rocks me, this kid."

"Yeah?" Marianne said. "Listen, I've got a new job, how about that? I'm working for Mac."

"And the lunch hour is over," I said. "Drop you somewhere, Nicky?"

I couldn't see his white teeth any more.

"No hurry," he said. "What kind of work, kid?"

"Research," she said.

Nicky came along with us to the street.

"What kind of research?"

"I'm writing a book about Steel City," I said.

"What do you know?"

I picked three newspapers off the rack. Nicky took a match out of his mouth and waved it at me.

"I know some stuff about Steel City," he said, "that you won't find in the papers. I could write a book myself."

"Where can I get in touch with you?" I said.

"I'll be around. Marianne knows where I am."

"The right kind of information is worth money to me," I said. He nodded, shrugging and twitching and tossed his match into the gutter. I led Marianne to a waiting cab. When I looked back, Nicky was standing in the depot entrance, watching us go. "What was it about having your tonsils out?" I asked her.

"What—? Oh, you mean Nicky. It's all right to tell Nicky. He's my friend. He wouldn't talk to cops. He hates cops."

"Then everything's all right."

"Sure."

I told the driver to go here and there and after a few blocks, stopped him at a streetside telephone booth.

"You had a call to make," I said. I gave her the change for it. "Somebody to work for you?"

"Oh, yeah. Charlene, I guess."

She got out and went into the booth and we waited about five minutes. She came back fuming.

"That bitch Charlene! All my tips for a week!"

"How much do you make in tips?"

"Fifteen, maybe twenty dollars."

"I'll make it up to you."

"I never saw such a stingy character."

I got her into the cab.

* * * *

The Broadview Apartments were stacked in a brick building on a semi-commercial street. From a window we could see the old courthouse. Beyond it and looming above was the Prescott Hotel. So at least everything was well centralized. If nothing should come of it, we wouldn't have a long trip home.

The apartment had a bedroom, dressing room, kitchen and living room. It was nothing much and it made that kind of impression. Marianne put her feet on the coffee table and brooded.

"When do I start?" she said. "What do I do?"

"Nothing now. I'll be out for a while."

"You're not going to stay here?"

"I'll be in and out. You'll be safe here. Just don't let anybody in."

"Nobody?"

"Nobody, including Nicky."

"What's wrong? You jealous of Nicky because he hangs around with me?"

"Uh-huh," I said. "I guess that's it."

I turned on a couple of lamps and went into the bedroom and turned down her bed. She followed me around like a kitten, never too close, never far away. I turned on the heater in the bathroom.

"Big bed," I said, "all yours. Take a long, hot bath and crawl in, sleep like a baby."

"What'll I do when I wake up?"

"Read the papers. I'll be back. Remember, we're signed in here as Robert Berry and daughter, Mary Ann. Think of me as your father."

She looked at me speculatively.

"It could be," she said. "You're old enough."

"So there's nothing to it. What size are you?"

"What?"

"I'll get you some things to wear. What size?"

"Small. The smallest. Don't get yellow. I hate yellow."

On the way to the door, I picked up the telephone. The landlady had offered to have it connected and I had declined. The line was dead. So she wouldn't be calling any of her happy friends to pass the time of day.

As I reached to open the door, she ran in from the dressing room. She had kicked off the sandals and the top of her head was in line with my breast pocket. Her pinched face was deeply troubled.

"I don't know anything about you," she said. "You talk about money and all—have you got any?"

I got out my wallet and let her look at the hundred-dollar bill Karen had given me earlier that day. Her eyes widened.

"Maybe an advance can be arranged," I said. "Will you answer a question?"

"Maybe."

"What size are your shoes?"

"Three. You're nuts."

"Let's try another one. You told me this morning you were born at Green Acres."

"I was! My mother was working there, for Mrs. Lloyd. My father was there too."

"That would be your real father, not Deacon Roberts?"

"The Deacon was only my stepfather. My real father died a long time ago."

"When were you born?"

"December fourteenth, nineteen thirty-five."

"You're sure of it?"

"I guess I know my own birthday!"

"All right," I said, "I guess you'll earn your way."

I pulled the bill out of my wallet. That snapshot of her was in there with it and came out at the same time. I missed catching it and it fell on the floor face up. She was the kind who noticed things. Slowly she stooped, saw what it was, lifted it.

"Where did you get this?" Her eyes were claws on my face. "Is that what you want with me—you—?"

"No, it isn't. I happened to have that—"

She shook the snapshot in my face viciously.

"I never did this! Just because that Pete Bowman—"

"No! Don't give me that, Marianne. Pete didn't do it. Your dear friend Connie did it."

Her mouth was open, but she kept it quiet.

"Connie tricked you into this, all by herself."

"She was only fooling—"

"All right. You can have the picture. I don't want it."

I slapped the hundred into her hand and she held onto it. As quickly as it had come, her hostility faded. She yawned in my face. When I went out she was standing there clutching the bill, looking confused...

* * * *

I rode the taxi to the bus depot and switched to my car. At the hotel desk I rented a room and cashed a check for two hundred dollars. Off the lobby I found a women's wear salon and a petite salesgirl with a friendly disposition.

"If you were smaller than you are," I said, "and wore size three shoes and if you were stuck for the weekend for apparel—a couple of dresses, stockings, nightgown—what would you buy?"

"Well, I—smaller than me?—that's small."

"Yes. Very small."

"I don't know, I'd want—"

"Will you pick them out for me and send them to my room, please?"

"Of course, but—"

"I'm sure your taste is flawless. Don't be stingy with yourself. On the other hand, you're not going to any fancy-dress balls."

"If you say so—"

I left it to her and started across the lobby. I didn't quite make the elevator. Two well-set-up fellows in hats and chain-store suits contrived quietly to block my way. The older one did the talking.

"Lieutenant Sharp," he said. "I think you've met Sergeant Downs."

We nodded all around.

"My place or yours?" I asked.

"We've got a car right outside," the Lieutenant said.

"Then by all means."

They flanked me all the way, walking and riding and walking some more till we came to a quiet room in a busy municipal building where the only instrument of torture was a ventilating fan that squeaked. I got so I didn't notice it much.

CHAPTER EIGHTEEN

The discussion began with some opening remarks by Lieutenant Sharp. He had a name that fit him real tight. His face was lean, angular, with a long-ish nose and close-set eyes. He was young for a lieutenant, maybe forty-five. He had unruly hair that he kept brushing back from his forehead. He was on the gloomy side.

"Let's get a couple of things clear," he said. "In this town, the police and the Green Acres people work hand in glove. We know they're on the level. But you are a private eye from Chicago and we don't know any such thing about you. So don't start with the idea that you are under the protection of Green Acres. Maybe you were smart to go to them first, maybe not. The thing to remember is, you're on your own here."

"All right," I said.

"The other thing is that I don't know why you came to town, but if you had the idea of hanging a local policeman, the sooner you shake it, the better. We don't cover up, but we clean our own house."

I loosened my tie and rubbed my neck. The armless chair was very hard, the room overwarm. Considering the leisurely pace established by the Lieutenant, the thing could go on for a long time.

"Sure," I said. "Go ahead."

"Tell us how you happened to find Bowman?"

I told them exactly as I had told Prince. I put Karen Bowman in as my employer and left Marianne out. It took me about ten minutes. When I finished, the Lieutenant got up and walked around.

"How long were you in the cottage?" he asked.

"Five minutes, six or seven."

"Then after you talked to Mr. Lloyd in the boat, what did you do?"

"I drove downtown."

"Why?" he said quickly. "If you were going to make the notification through Green Acres?"

"At first I planned to come here and notify you directly, in person."

"Why in person?"

"So it wouldn't go through your switchboard."

"How come that?" Sergeant Downs said.

"Come on," I said. "If the President of the United States or some member of his family should die of a gunshot wound and whoever discovered the body knew his identity, would he grab the nearest telephone and start blabbing?"

"Peter Bowman wasn't the President," Sharp said.

"He was the son-in-law of Calvin Lloyd, and it could have been suicide, and I was working for his wife."

"You did a lot of figuring."

"I make a living."

"What were you going to do if Mrs. Bowman hadn't reached Green Acres? Just wait?"

"No. I'd have told Prince or Mr. Lloyd."

"You're some name dropper," Downs said.

The Lieutenant's question overrode Downs's crack. I saw the Sergeant's face go pink.

"Get back to the cottage," Sharp said. "You notice the gloves Bowman was wearing?"

I loosened the buttons at the top of my shirt.

"No, I didn't," I said.

"Good eyes. He wasn't wearing gloves."

"As I remember."

"You think he shot himself by accident? Or a suicide?"

"It looked that way."

"Then how do you suppose it happened his fingerprints weren't on the gun?"

"Weren't they?"

"No, nor anybody else's. The gun was as clean as a trout stream. That mean anything to you?"

"It means he was murdered, possibly by another gun."

"We'll know about the gun pretty soon. Let's talk about what else it means. It might mean that somebody came along and wiped the gun clean before we were notified."

"Somebody like me."

"Like you."

"Or whoever shot him at some earlier time."

"What earlier time? Do you know?"

"At a rough guess, it was between eight o'clock last evening and midnight. Give or take a couple of hours."

"Okay," Sharp said, "what about it?"

"Nothing except that I can pretty well account for my time up to six this morning."

"Suppose you do that," he said.

"From about eight-thirty to midnight I was with Lieutenant Donovan, Chicago, who was investigating the murder of Deacon Roberts. From shortly after midnight until about two-thirty, I was with Mrs. Bowman in Chicago. I checked with my answering service from my Chicago office about five o'clock. I started for Steel City at five-fifteen. It took me two hours."

"Seven o'clock," Downs said.

"What about between two-thirty and four o'clock this morning?" Sharp asked.

"I slept. Anyway, I couldn't have made the round trip in two and a half hours."

"Suppose Bowman was shot after seven o'clock?"

"If you find that he was," I said, "I guess we'll have to go through this again. But you won't and you must know it."

They should have had a fast comeback for that but either they didn't or they were withholding it. Without warning, they started out of the room. The Lieutenant spoke from the door.

"Don't go away," he said.

I sat around. The room grew warmer by the minute. I took off my coat and tie and hung them over the back of the chair. There were three large windows along a waist-high sill, all closed. I tried to open each one and decided that by official rule, they were opened for the summer on Memorial Day and closed on Labor Day for the winter.

They overlooked a parking lot, about one third of which was reserved for the police. It was neither crowded nor bustling. A group of civil service people straggled back from the lunch hour, entering the building in pairs, trios, singly. I watched for a while and was about to turn away when a shiny red station wagon swung into the police lot and worked into a space near the building. In green letters on the door were the words: "Green Acres." The driver climbed out and it was Ward Prince. He started around the car, then halted and crawled in under the wheel. Sergeant Downs opened the near door and got in beside him. He sat with one foot hanging out through the open door. I'd have given several teeth for a skilled lip reader and a pair of binoculars, but the wish was sterile.

By my watch, they sat together for twelve minutes. Then the Sergeant got out and closed the door and Prince started out of the lot. At the street he braked suddenly, and a slight figure ran to the driver's side of the car. There was another brief dialogue before the station wagon went on into the street and disappeared. The owner of the slight figure watched it go and walked off slowly. I didn't need binoculars to see that it was Nicky Royal.

There were half a dozen chairs in the room and I tried each in turn. Each was harder than the one before. There was a heavily built, long conference table, its edges notched by the burning of countless cigarette butts. It was dusty, but you can't have everything even in City Hall. I stretched out on it and looked at the ceiling and the next thing I knew, I was studying the clean-cut face of Sergeant Downs and it was three o'clock in the afternoon.

"Come on," he said. "The Lieutenant wants you."

I slid out from under his face carefully. We were alone in the room and I had been in a position in which he might have abused me painfully. But either he had forgotten his beef, or he had orders to bring me in unmarked.

I got into my jacket and put my tie in my pocket. At the door, he gave me what could be described as a moderately searching look.

"You happen to know anything about the whereabouts of a girl named Marianne McLeod?" he said.

"No," I said. "Local girl?"

"You know nothing about her?"

"Nothing."

He worked on my eyes for a while, then opened the door and let me out. I followed him down a corridor to a door marked "Homicide Investigation—H. D. Sharp, Lt." There was an outer office with files and a middle-aged stenographer and beyond it a larger room containing a desk, another big table and Lieutenant Sharp. He looked at me moodily.

"Pete Bowman was a good friend of Charles Traven," he said.

"I guess so."

"You got any weird notions about trying to clear Traven's name?"

"Weird notions?"

"It would be a waste of time," he said. "We had Traven dead to rights."

"Part of that anyway," I said. "The dead part."

The Sergeant got the hurt moose look.

"You watch that lip, sonny."

"One thing seems clear," I said. "Traven couldn't have killed Bowman."

"Traven would have got the chair," Lieutenant Sharp said stubbornly. "I know it."

"All right, Lieutenant," I said, "but the fact remains that in my judgment, Traven could have been brought in alive."

His door opened and the stenographer came in with a half-sheet of flimsy. Sharp read its message and dropped it on his desk. "Bowman was shot by his own gun," he said. "That rifle."

I waited at the door and he shrugged and turned away.

"So," he said, "I guess he must have worn gloves while he did it and then took them off later."

"Uh-huh," I said. "Well, you know where to find me."

"I hope so," he said.

The Sergeant was studying his fingernails. I let myself out. The ghost of the unasked question went with me.

Why didn't the Lieutenant ask about Marianne? I kept thinking. Why only the Sergeant?

CHAPTER NINETEEN

In my room were a dozen packages from the dress shop, including a pair of suit boxes and two shoe boxes. Hose, lingerie and incidentals were individually wrapped in cellophane. In the suit boxes I found two plain, smart frocks, one blue and one green. There were two pairs of ballet slippers, blue and green. I put the blue shoes in the suit box with the blue dress. I put in one pair of hose, one slip and one panty girdle with supporters. I leaned the box against the wall by the door and packed the rest of the things in my traveling bag.

I got out the bar tab I'd found in Pete's wallet and reread it. If "Vit. Stat." meant "vital statistics," the "Mr. Crowley" part could refer to a newspaper employee, a mail advertising man or a records official at the courthouse.

I called the two daily newspapers in town and kept them working until they were positive they employed nobody named Crowley, even in the pressroom. I called the courthouse and asked for Mr. Crowley in the Vital Statistics Bureau. There was no Mr. Crowley. I opened the classified directory to the "Advertising" headings and started down the lists. There was no Crowley. But under "Advertising—Direct Mail," I found a possible lead.

"Name-All Accurate List Service," it read. "Personal—Specials—Vital Statistics." There were three other mailing-list services, but I recognized two of them as national firms which would be unlikely prospects from what I guessed was Bowman's point of view. The third was a woman's name that bore no resemblance to Crowley. I wrote down the address of the "Name-All" list service.

I found the torn letter addressed to Pete and laid the two halves together. It read:

Dear Mr. Bowman.

Re your inquiry regarding the estate of Anita McLeod Roberts, I beg to advise that my connection with this account was terminated upon Mrs. Roberts' death in 1953. I have no information as to the disposition of such assets as may have existed at the time. Nor do I know anything of her daughter, who, I believe, would be the only blood relative with a direct claim on the estate, if there should be any substance worth claiming.

For further information, you might inquire of a Mrs. Constance Traven, who was, I believe, a close friend of Mrs. Roberts and who was living with her at the time of her death.

Very truly yours,

Abbott Farrell, C. P. A.

The letter was about as helpful as an obituary and it was easy to see why Pete had thrown it away. I had a similar impulse. But I also had Marianne—in a way—so I was in much the same position Pete must have been in when Marianne went to the cottage to see him. I was maybe even a little ahead.

The switchboard operator had some trouble making a connection with my meticulous informant in Chicago. Not because he wasn't in; he answered readily. The operator gave him my name and said I was calling from the Prescott Hotel.

"One moment," he said. "How is that spelled?"

"How is what spelled?" the operator said.

"The Hotel Prescott, was that it?"

"That's what I—"

"Spell it, please."

She spelled it, biting every letter.

"And the telephone number?"

She gave it to him.

"Would you like to speak to your party now?" she asked warily.

"Thank you," he said, and hung up.

The operator made a sound in her throat.

"It's all right," I said. "He'll call back."

"Look, if this is some trick to chisel the telephone company—"

"No," I said. "He's a little absent-minded. If he hasn't called back in five minutes, place the call again."

"Well, I never—" An incoming call drew her away. It would have been impossible in the time allotted me to explain him to her as he had explained himself to me.

"You see, Mac, this is a pretty dull way to make a living—digging up unrelated information, never knowing what significance it has, what it may lead to. You might be tracking down a desperate psycho, or trying to spot a hidden bomb in Comiskey Park; or you may be tracing some deadbeat who owes fifteen dollars at the corner drugstore. The thing is, I never get to know. I accept this intellectually, but emotionally it's frustrating as hell. Life without excitement is like skim milk or near beer, nutritious but innocuous. So I put the excitement in myself by making each case mysterious, pregnant with hidden meaning. Besides, I love cryptograms with a fierce passion. It takes longer that way, but it's more fun. Do you begrudge me?"

The only thing he had appeared to overlook was the fact that I had to pay the telephone bills. Still, they were deductible and I couldn't begrudge him.

When he called back, he got right to business.

"I have your material," he said in his dry monotone. "As to the best manner of transmittal—"

I jumped in fast.

"Let's just use the simple step-up," I said. "By one."

"Well, I thought perhaps a switchback midway—"

"I think the other will suffice."

"Very well." He was disappointed. He'd have preferred to give it to me in the symbols of nuclear physics, so I should spend a week at Los Alamos getting it deciphered. "Attention all pencils."

He started in and I dutifully wrote it down. By holding him to the "single step-up" I needed only to read for each letter or number the one that preceded it in the alphabet or list of numbers. ANITA MCLEOD became BOJUB NDMFPE, BOX became CPY, and so on down the list. The whole thing took about five minutes. When he finished and wanted to check it with me, I said, "Look, if you're on commission with the A. T. & T., I don't want to break up a good thing, but—"

"Oh," he said abruptly. "I assumed you were on an expense account."

He hung up. I deciphered his nonsense syllables on another sheet of paper and what I came up with read like this:

> Second Natl. Bank 42 Chicago Box 302—Anita McLeod—Feb. 15, 1940 to Sept. 30, 1950
> Anita McLeod Roberts/Constance Waters jointly, Oct. 1, 1950 to Dec. 19, 1952.
> Constance Waters Traven, Dec. 20, 1952 to present cont.
> Box 516—Lilian W. Carmichael, Dec. 20, 1952 to April 8, 1957.

I fooled around with my pencil, making another juxtaposition of part of the data. It came out like this:

> Box 302—Constance W. Traven, Dec. 20, 1952 to present.
> Box 516—Lilian W. Carmichael, Dec. 20, 1952 to April 8, 1957.
> Constance Traven deceased April 6, 1957. Saturday.

I looked at all this for a while. Then I picked up the letter from Abbott Farrell to Pete Bowman, read it through, tore Farrell's address off the letterhead and put it in my pocket along with the address of the Name-All List Service. I picked up the suit box with Marianne's new wardrobe in it and left the room and the hotel. It was four o'clock and I had about an hour of the business day left.

I wasted ten minutes of it trying to shake a police shadow that didn't exist. When I found for certain they had nobody on me, it made me more nervous than if it had been true. The thought that they might already have found her had me panting at the apartment door.

The sight of her sound asleep in bed with the covers up to her chin was a relief, but it didn't eliminate my worry. They ought to be out looking for her. They ought to be out following me.

I laid the suit box on a chair beside the bed where she would see it when she woke. I looked at her child's face, relaxed in sleep. The edges of her short cropped hair were damp. Her face was clean and there was the fragrance of soap about her. There was no sign of the snapshot I had turned over to her. I looked around for Connie's photograph and it appeared to have suffered a loss of esteem. It had not been set up on the bureau, but was lying on the bed, face up, partially covered by her discarded sweater. After a minute I left, tiptoeing away so as not to waken her.

CHAPTER TWENTY

In the front yard of a small frame house on the edge of the main business district, a weather-beaten sign read: NAME-ALL LIST SERVICE, and in smaller letters below, R.N. CROWLEY. A white card over the doorbell read: "Ring and Enter."

A massive desk was stacked with runaway stacks of paper stapled in sheaves. Beyond, through an open door, I saw a workroom with shelves and a duplicating machine. On a corner of the desk not covered by papers lay a sleeping calico cat.

The man at the desk was portly, with a tuft of white hair on each side of his head and none in between. He wore a green eyeshade and a pair of horn-rimmed glasses that kept slipping down on his nose. His complexion was that of a spottily faded beet, but his face was genial when he greeted me.

"Richard Crowley at your service. Sit down, sir." I sat down. "What can I do for you?"

"I'm not sure—"

"Something in a list, Mr.—?"

I gave him my name and it didn't produce any special reaction. He nodded and launched an immediate pitch, as glib as I had ever heard.

"Been in this business twenty years. You'd be surprised how useful this service has been to many firms. Yes, sir. The list is the lifeblood of direct-mail selling, simple as that. Suppose you want to reach home owners in the fourteen-five to twenty-eight bracket. Nothing easier."

His gears were in perfect mesh. He rose with dignity to face me across the desk.

"You may say, 'This is public information, available in any courthouse; why shouldn't I make my own list?' A sound question. But consider the time element, starting from scratch. Three thousand homes in this county alone, name and address, at top speed you could jot down three hundred per hour. Ten hours' time, sir! Yours or a paid assistant's. My files and index system enable me to prepare such a list, complete and ready for use, within two hours at the outside."

"It would be foolish for me try it," I said.

"It would be costly, sir. Let's put it that way."

"All right. You also deal in vital statistics, I understand."

"True. Birth, marriage, death—the cycle of life, if I may say so. Can't compete with the city folks, of course. But anywhere else in the state. No national list service can meet my price, except on a national basis."

I expressed admiration at his lack of grandiose ambition.

"I try to fill my niche," he said. "No more and no less. May I ask who referred you to me?"

"A friend of mine—Peter Bowman, an attorney."

"Oh, Mr. Bowman! He was in here only yesterday. Curious affair—" He frowned, sat down slowly and leaned back in his swivel chair.

"I may say it's the first time in my experience—but, no matter. Mustn't take your time."

"Please go on," I said. "You must know some fascinating stories about this country."

He seemed pleased.

"For that matter, the whole state," he said. "Traveled it up and down, mile by mile. Many years ago. Selling. Drummers they called us then. Sold everything from pots and pans to diamond watches. Sold Bibles. Had a heart attack, had to ease off, drifted into this business. What business are you in, if I may ask?"

"Real estate," I said. "Chicago. Pete Bowman has handled some legal work for me."

"Seems like a fine fellow. Shrewd."

"He told me something about this thing he's been on here—some estate—Roberts, McLeod, something. He said there was a girl named Marianne he was trying to locate—"

"Marianne McLeod. Oh, I think he knew where she was all right. Matter of establishing her birth. As I said, a very curious thing."

"I should think a birth could be established easily. After all, either you are or you never were."

"Man would think so," he said gravely. "Well, sir, Mr. Bowman had been to the courthouse and found no record of this girl's birth. He came to me—I'm sometimes referred to as 'the poor man's Hall of Records.' He had a birth date for the young woman, and in checking back, I found sure enough I had her name on a birth list. One of my earliest efforts. Plain as day." He rifled through some papers, drew out a single sheet, dusty and brittle with age. "Have it right here, still legible."

When I reached for it, he held back, then said, "You seem to know about it. Mr. Bowman said nothing about keeping it to myself—"

Halfway down the page I found the name, "McLeod, Marianne—Dec. 14. M—Anita McLeod. Green Acres." Then there was the name "Royal" and the letters "BOW." I glanced at Crowley and he pursed his lips sadly.

"Born out of wedlock, of course. Regrettable. Nowadays they don't put that on the basic certificate."

"This 'Royal,'" I said, "is the doctor's name?"

He chuckled, shook his head.

"Years ago we had a midwife here, Kate Royal. Colorful character. Got in some trouble. Moved away long ago."

"Miss Royal was it?"

"Mrs. Husband worked on the railroad. Killed under a train."

"Did Mrs. Royal have any children of her own?"

"Don't rightly remember. But to get back to the curious thing about this Miss McLeod—my only source for this information is the courthouse. Now I've made mistakes in my time—misspellings, incorrect dates, once in a while an omission. But I'd swear I never wrote down a listing like this if it never existed. If I hadn't seen it, it wouldn't be there. And the only place I could have seen it was the courthouse."

"And you say Pete Bowman couldn't find it at the courthouse?"

"No, sir, and neither could I. I checked on it myself. They had no record whatsoever on this birth. They had a record for every other name on that page. But not for this one."

I handed the sheet back to him.

"Would it be possible to steal an original document like this from your courthouse?"

"Oh, it might. But it wouldn't have any value. The value of a birth certificate is that it's backed up by the original in the courthouse. Wouldn't be worth the risk, to try and steal it."

"I suppose not—unless you wanted to erase the record, so that the subject could never prove his identity."

He looked at me solemnly.

"I sat right where I'm sitting now and told Mr. Bowman the same thing," he said. "I was all for putting it up to the county people right now."

"But Mr. Bowman didn't want that?"

"No. Decent sort of fellow. Said the destruction of public records is a serious offense and he didn't want to embarrass anyone till he'd done some more checking."

"Did he mention any particular person he wanted not to embarrass? Any institution?"

"No, he didn't."

"I suppose you've come to know a lot of the county employees in your time."

"When it comes to records, yes, I have."

"People hang onto these jobs for years. Take the Vital Statistics Bureau—is the same person in charge now who was there when you went into business? Clerk, recorder, whatever he is?"

"No, sir. The chief clerk in that department when I started was an old duffer named Sam Galloway. You noticed on that list the name of Green Acres? Well, Sam was a good example of what Green Acres means to people around here."

"I'd like to hear about Sam."

"Sam was an honest, hard-working citizen—civic minded, all that. But he had a son that went wrong. In trouble from the time he was a kid. When he was eighteen, he got in real bad trouble. Held up a filling station with two others. A man was killed. Nearly finished Sam off.

"Well, the kid got let off on the killing but was sent up for the robbery. He came out about the time Mr. Lloyd was getting Green Acres organized. It must have been that Sam went out to see Mr. Lloyd personally, because when his boy came out of prison, he was paroled to Green Acres. And you can believe it or not—he straightened out! Three years there and he was a different fellow. He now has one of the finest farms in this county, a wife and three grown children. Too bad Sam only got to see the start of it."

"Sam is no longer living?"

"Passed away twelve, thirteen years ago. Retired from the civil service shortly after his boy went to Green Acres. I got along fine with Sam. But he was a sick man for years. Something to do with his boy's trouble I suppose."

I picked up my hat and got on my feet.

"So Sam Galloway knew he was going to die before he retired from his job at the courthouse."

"Sure he did."

He had said it off the top of his head. I saw him go stiff and his face turned slowly to mine.

"What was that again?"

I backed away.

"You ain't in the real estate business," he said.

"In a way—"

"You didn't come in here to buy a mailing list."

"Not exactly."

"You're some kind of cop."

"I've been working for Pete Bowman—"

"Pretty smart, ain't you?"

I got to the door.

"I hope someday," I said, "you can say that and mean it."

I got out. It was still daylight, but heavy clouds had come up and a damp, driving wind.

CHAPTER TWENTY-ONE

The *"e"* in Abbott Farrell's name on the old directory had disappeared. Most of the other letters stood at odd angles on the gray-black board in the lobby of the walk-up office building.

On his door were the words "Abbott Farrell, Public Accountant, C. P. A." The letters were intact and the glass had been recently cleaned. A decal in the lower left corner proclaimed that the premises were protected by William J. Burns Detective Agency.

There was a large oak desk littered with papers, an accountant's work sheets and a stack of heavily bound ledgers with frayed edges. On a portable stand was an adding machine about twenty years old. If there was anyone at the desk, he was hidden by the ledgers, and the stack wasn't a high one.

I stood in the doorway and waited and a face looked around the ledgers, a small, multi-lined face with small, bright eyes.

"Mr. Farrell?" I said.

He nodded acknowledgment.

"Be with you in a minute," he said.

At closer range, before lowering myself into an ancient, comfortable armchair, I saw that, physically, in relation to the ledgers and the big desk, Mr. Farrell was at some disadvantage. Stunted by a spinal deformity, he was unable when seated either to reach the floor with his feet or to look across the low stack of ledgers. He had the ageless face of the malformed.

He was running down a column, reaching with his left hand to operate the machine by a touch system I didn't doubt was totally accurate. I had time to reflect on the probability that a CPA who had stayed in business for himself for more than twenty years was not only competent but incorruptible.

He pushed the machine away, made a notation and leaned back in his chair. The way he swung it about with no straining of his torso convinced me he had installed a platform for his feet. "Now then," he said.

I told him my name and profession. He frowned.

"You must know," he said, "I can't give you any information about my accounts."

"I'm interested in an account that is now defunct," I said. "I'm not collecting a bill."

"Whom do you represent?"

"A Marianne McLeod, daughter of Anita McLeod."

"I see."

"You did some accounting for Mrs. Roberts."

"I prepared tax returns for her over a period of fifteen years."

"Those returns, pretty complex, were they?"

"Not especially."

"Did she have a substantial income?"

"I can't discuss that," he said.

"But your client is dead."

"Nevertheless."

"All right. How about Constance Traven, or Constance Waters? Did you know her?"

"A friend of Mrs. Roberts. I met her."

"More than once?"

"Two or three times. She came with Mrs. Roberts twice to the office."

"Went over finances with her?"

"They seemed very close. Mrs. Roberts wasn't well. Miss Waters seemed to be considerate and helpful."

"Did you see Miss Waters at other times?"

"Once, shortly after Mrs. Roberts' death. I called to inquire about a tax return for the year in which she died. Miss Waters said she was making other arrangements."

"That was the last you saw of Miss Waters?"

"Yes."

"And the end of any connection you had with Mrs. Roberts' financial affairs?"

"Well, about six months after that, I received an informal inquiry from the Internal Revenue people regarding Mrs. Roberts' estate."

"Did she have an estate?"

"I didn't know. I referred them to her husband."

"Deacon Roberts?"

"Yes. He was in prison at the time."

"Did they get their answer?"

"I don't know."

I got up and filled my lungs. I had the sensation of being chased again, but I had to get more out of Mr. Farrell. He had come this far with me only because, with the one slight exception, we hadn't touched on anything involving his professional integrity. I had got up from restlessness and not with any idea of impressing him with my physique. But for a moment, when I turned to him, I caught him looking at me with an odd, hungry look. His eyes shifted at once, but I had seen it. Still, I didn't sit down, but stayed on my feet, high above him.

"What does your client want?" he said, breaking the bad silence. "Money? The inheritance—?"

"If Anita left anything," I said, "Marianne would be entitled to it, wouldn't she?"

"I suppose she would."

"Is there any, Mr. Farrell?"

"I don't know."

"But you have reason to suspect there is."

He looked me full in the face for a count of five and I knew he had come to the end of the line. I felt no resentment. The stubborn pride of men like him is about all that stands between the ordinary working person and disaster.

"I'm afraid we'll have to terminate this," he said. "I'm very busy." He picked up a pencil.

I gave him a minute to get his things in order. I closed off a certain area of my conscious mind. I leaned across his big desk and found his honest eyes.

"Mr. Farrell," I said, "some people in the world are more handicapped than others. Among the handicapped, it shows in different ways. If you've never seen her, you'll have to take my word—it shows in Marianne McLeod. I think I can help her, if I can get certain information. I think she has it coming."

His face might have been molded of wet ashes. I did it again. "Believe me," I said, "it shows; just as much as if she had a physical deformity."

With slow precision, he set his pencil point on the desk and ran his finger and thumb down its length till it toppled of its own weight.

"What do you want?" he said harshly.

"Anita McLeod had a sizable income, didn't she?"

"Quite."

"Did she work? Did she have a job?"

"Off and on, some menial work."

"Did she have a checking account?"

"No. I suggested it. She was a very simple person, with a lot of fears."

"Was she extravagant?"

"On the contrary. She spent less than half her income."

"What was the source of her income?"

"It was a paid-up annuity. Twenty years."

"Did she ever tell you who had paid it?"

"No. I saw one of the checks once. It was drawn on an Eastern bank. There was no designation on it other than her name."

"How big a check was it?"

"More than five hundred dollars."

"For the one month?"

"Yes."

"And she spent only half of it."

"That would be my rough guess."

"Then over twenty years, she should have saved up over fifty thousand dollars."

"Roughly, yes."

"You say she would get these checks and cash them? Everything cash?"

"That was my understanding."

"Where would she keep the cash?"

"What she used, I suppose she kept on her person. The excess, I don't know."

"Is that what the Internal Revenue people were looking for? That residue of cash?"

"I think so."

"Did they ever find it?"

"I think not."

I stared at him and he stared back, expressionless.

"Mr. Farrell," I said, "if you were my financial adviser and I told you I was sharing a safe deposit box full of fifty thousand dollars with a friend, in joint tenancy—what would be your opinion of my judgment?"

"It would depend," he said, "on your objective and on your competence."

"Competence?"

"You didn't know Anita McLeod. The last two or three times she came here, twice with Miss Waters, she was very ill. I remember asking whether she had made any provision for her daughter and Miss Waters interrupted and explained it was all taken care of. Then Miss McLeod—Mrs. Roberts—said yes, that Miss Waters would see that Marianne was take care of."

"And you didn't follow that up?"

"After the last meeting with Mrs. Roberts, it was out of my hands."

I straightened and turned. His fingers drummed a slow dirge on the adding machine keys.

"Did you ever hear of a Mrs. Lilian W. Carmichael?" I asked.

"No," he said dully. "Will that be all now?"

I couldn't quite look at him. I went to the door and hung around and finally went through it.

"Thanks," I said. "I'm sorry."

He didn't say anything. I went out quickly and down the old hall and the old steps and outside. I leaned over the gutter and spat for a while, but the bad taste lingered.

Who is corrupt now? I thought; who the corrupter?

The dingy question haunted me all the way to the hotel. It haunted me through a quick shower and shave and the time it took to pack my bag and check out of the hotel. It rode me, a minute jockey with spurs, to the morgue of the older of the city's two daily papers, where an aging attendant took the name "Kate Royal" under advisement and eventually directed me to a fifteen-year-old bound volume of the Steel City *Banner*.

The story was brief and inconspicuous. An illegal operation case against Mrs. Royal had been stopped short of trial when the charge was withdrawn by an unnamed complainant. There was a picture of Mrs. Royal in a hospital bed with a dour-faced woman in street clothes standing beside it.

"Mrs. Royal," the report concluded, "mother of a five-year-old son, has been in ill health since the death of her husband in a railroad accident three years ago. She was released from the detention ward of County Hospital in the care of a sister, Mrs. Wilton Parker, of Decatur."

It wasn't much, but maybe enough, with what I had, and the cleanest way to wrap it up would be, certainly, the most direct.

In a phone booth in the lobby, I dialed Green Acres. When I asked the male switchboard operator if I could speak to Mr. Lloyd, his first response was a full minute of eloquent silence.

"Mr. Lloyd hasn't spoken on the telephone for fifteen years," he said.

I asked for Ward Prince.

"I'm sorry, he's not in," he said.

I asked for Mrs. Bowman.

"I'll see," he said. Then, a minute later, "Mrs. Bowman doesn't answer. Will you leave your number?"

I hung up. There was no time to chat with him, whoever he was in his niche on the safe side of the big gate. It was well past dark and Marianne would be hungry.

* * * *

I drove a block and a half beyond the apartment and walked back. It had been raining and now it had stopped, but the cold, driving wind persisted. The foyer was deserted. I climbed the stairs and went to our door and after a while I found my key.

The living room was dark. I flipped the switch and she wasn't there. In the bedroom, the bed was empty. All her clothes were gone, including those I had bought her. The picture of Connie Traven still lay on the bed, but face down now. I looked in the bathroom. I looked around for a note.

On the floor in the living room was a late racing form. Under the useless telephone was a local directory. I got it open to the "*Rs*."

"Royal, Nick," the listing read. "51 Pine Lake Road."

I turned off the light and left the place.

CHAPTER TWENTY-TWO

Unless moonshining was part of his activities, a dilapidated farmhouse eight miles from town seemed an unlikely place for Nicky to live. On the other hand, it was within a stone's throw of Green Acres, and that fit, and the attendant at the filling station where Pine Lake Road intersected the highway had assured me that this was the right spot. The name "Royal" showed on a leaning mailbox beside a narrow lane. Wet branches slapped at my face as I made my way past a red sports car parked just off the road.

The rundown house was lighted and shades had been drawn on all the windows, but one was ragged at the bottom and I could look into the front room. The two of them were seated at an old-fashioned round dining table. The suit box I had delivered to the apartment was on the table, apparently still unopened. Marianne was dressed as earlier. There was a bottle of her favorite beverage in front of her. Across from her sat Nicky with a bottle of beer. They were talking sporadically, but I could hear none of it above the sound of the wind. There was a slight list to the table top and it gave me a squeamish feeling.

In a corner, a shotgun leaned, well out of reach. I had no way of knowing what, if anything, Nicky might have on his person. Marianne's lips said something and there was no answer. She ran her fingers through her thin hair.

I went around to the front porch and managed to get onto it without banging anything. The rain-soaked boards were slick under my feet. The screen was closed and the shade had been drawn on the door. If it was locked, I was in trouble. I eased the screen open and if it squeaked, I couldn't hear it for the wind. I got my hand on the doorknob and twisted it silently, then pushed with my shoulder. It wasn't locked. I walked into the room, blinking in the sudden light.

Nicky swung around to face me, but stayed seated. Marianne jumped, startled, but kept quiet.

"Nicky boy," I said.

He grinned twitchily. I wondered how long it would take him to develop a permanent tic.

"Hi," he said. "How you coming with the research?"

"I don't know. I seem to have lost my assistant."

Marianne spoke up shrilly.

"You didn't come back. I thought you weren't coming. It was lonesome there—"

"I'm sorry," I said. I looked at Nicky again. "You found her in a hurry, but then I guess you know most of the cab drivers around town."

"Sure. Like I told you, I know a lot about this town. If you're interested in research."

"Listen, Mac," Marianne said, "Nicky brought me here to see Mr. Prince. He's the boss of Green Acres and he wants to see me. What's wrong with—"

"Shut up, kid," Nicky said.

"But Mr. Prince hasn't shown up yet," I said.

"He'll be here—" Nicky cut in calmly. "It just didn't seem right for Marianne to be shut up there all alone in a strange place with the cops looking for her and all that."

"I see. So you brought her to a safe place."

"Now you have got the idea."

I looked at Marianne and she met my eyes for a minute, then dropped them.

"Funny thing," I said. "I spent quite a lot of time with the police today and they never once mentioned Marianne."

Nicky spread his fingers on the table.

"Is that true, Mac?" Marianne said.

"So help me," I said.

Nicky got up slowly. The flicker of insolence at his mouth had changed to a wary tautness.

"Like she said," he droned, "we're expecting company and it's kind of a private thing. We've got nothing here for you."

"I don't know," I said, "you've got Marianne. She's a regular gold mine. Everybody wants her."

Marianne looked puzzled. If I could keep her puzzled, we were making progress. She got on her feet slowly and pondered Nicky's profile.

"You're pretty good," I said, "at whatever it is you do, but you're selling yourself out for nickels and dimes. Didn't Mr. Prince ever tell you what Marianne is really worth?"

He was fooling with his jacket sleeves, adjusting them carefully, especially the left one. I began watching the left one with interest.

"Maybe you didn't hear me," he said carefully. "I told you to get going."

I looked at Marianne till she met my eyes, then shrugged and turned away.

"If Marianne doesn't want the job I offered," I said, "it's up to her."

"Drop that, peeper," Nicky growled. "You got no job for her."

"Nicky," Marianne said, "he already gave me a hundred dollars—"

"Big deal," he snorted.

"I don't know, Nicky. He was all right to me. You didn't have any business coming around there—"

"Shut up," he said.

His eyes watched me move carelessly in a brief arc toward the door. Marianne's fingers toyed nervously with the string around the suit box.

"Go on," Nicky said. "Get out."

Marianne moved behind him.

"Wait a minute, I'm going with him—"

Nicky took a step backward.

"What?"

She moved closer, watching me.

Nicky had very good reflexes. I straightened against the door when his left jacket sleeve ejected an open knife. He pivoted, grabbed Marianne tightly, pinning her arms, and came out of it facing me with the knife close to her throat. Her greenish eyes went wide.

"Your big man friend is leaving," he said. "You stay quiet, kid." Her momentary fear became fury as if operated by a switch.

I saw her throat convulse.

"Nicky, you let go of me, you son-of-a-bitch—"

"Stand still, Marianne," I said. "Don't talk. Just stand still and he won't hurt you."

"No?" Nicky said.

"Huh-uh," I said. "Because if you do, I'll kill you. Right here with my hands and your own knife."

"Sure you will," he said.

"Don't read me wrong, Nicky. I'll kill you dead."

He held on for about thirty seconds while Marianne's eyes clawed at me. Then he swung her away and she reeled into the table. He lunged with the knife out, feinting, and pivoted, coming up closer but still out of my reach. My hands were shaking to get at him, but I had seen how fast he was.

"Come on," I said. "You yellow, Nicky? Would it make it easier if I would turn around? You're better from behind, huh?" That brought him. He came in a rush and I stepped back so that the knife stuck in the wooden jamb of the door and he jerked at it frantically. I hit his wrist with my right hand and pushed him away with my left. The knife thudded to the floor.

He looked up at me from a crouch. Most of his fight was gone. Marianne was edging wide around him.

"Let's go," I said.

She started, then ran back to the table, grabbed the suit box and brought it along, holding it awkwardly against her chest. I pushed the screen door open and backed out after her. Everything would have gone fine then, only

Marianne slipped on the wet boards and I tried to catch her. Then Nicky was coming out at me. I saw the flash of the knife in his hand but I was off balance against one of the posts. I twisted, but felt it go into me in the soft part of my shoulder and the searing wrench as he jerked it out to take another stab. I kicked him in the stomach and when he sagged, I hit him in the face and he went down on the porch.

I found Marianne huddled against the rail, clutching the box. There wasn't much feeling in the place he had stuck me. That would come later. I made sure he was down for a while and took Marianne's arm.

"Come on," I said, "the car's out in the road."

She came along silently, hugging that box. We plowed through the wet grass, stumbling in the ruts of the lane. A branch slapped at her and she swore under her breath.

At the car she held back.

"Where we going?"

I opened the door and gave her a push and she scrambled in under the wheel and across the seat. I got it started and drove straight down the road toward the lake.

"Was that true, about Ward Prince?" I asked.

"Sure. Mr. Prince talked to me on the phone. He said he would fix it for me to go to Green Acres."

"You want to go to Green Acres?"

"Who wouldn't?"

After a minute I asked her, "Did you bring your money with you?"

"What money?"

"The hundred dollars."

"No. I gave it to Nicky, to put on a horse."

The lake glistened on our left now. I felt the first driving pain in my shoulder.

"What was the horse's name?" I asked.

"Marianne."

My damp fingers slipped on the wheel and I tightened them spasmodically. I was a little afraid of her.

CHAPTER TWENTY-THREE

It was quiet and cold as a mausoleum. With the place closed up the way it was, I couldn't even hear the wind. Marianne sat on the edge of a slipcovered wing chair, hugging herself with both arms. I suppressed a cough, only to have it erupt on me a moment later. The spasm of pain in my torn shoulder turned the air bright with falling crystals.

"See if the stove is turned on," I said. "Open the oven and turn it way up."

She gazed at me blankly, then went to the kitchen, her thin shoulders hunched forward.

"I don't know how to turn it on," she called.

"Is there a pilot under the oven?"

"A what?"

"A pilot—a little blue flame—"

Christ, I thought.

"Never mind," I said. "Come in here."

She wandered into the room, staring at me, her lower lip trembling. Carefully, balancing my stiffening left arm on hip and thigh, I crowded over to the wall on the couch. I lifted a corner of the old blanket.

"Come on," I said.

She came like an automaton to the edge of the couch and stopped.

"What for?" she said.

"Just get in here where you'll be warm."

The crystals danced like crazy at the lurch of the springs as she crawled in beside me. I got my good arm around her and pulled her close and managed to work the blanket up to her neck. She was shivering and her tiny, fragile figure was like a bundle of loosely bound sticks against my shoulder and chest and flank. Her breath on my neck was hot and when her forehead brushed my cheek, it was feverish.

This will be one for the papers, I thought. When I bleed to death and she dies of pneumonia and they find us here—the brilliant private eye and the waif on parole in a dead man's rendezvous.

She stirred restlessly and her fingers played with a button on my jacket. She coughed a frail gust against my neck.

"Mac—"

"Yeah, honey?"

"Why do we have to stay here?"

"Because the huntsmen are up and I'm winged."

"What?"

I hugged her. It hurt both of us and she stiffened, holding back.

"Mac, I'm hungry."

"I know," I said. "It won't be long. All I need is a rest and for this thing to settle down and clot—" I stopped with the words, but the thoughts dribbled on.

...and maybe a place to go for the rest of my life if this doesn't come off...

She was lying on her back now and I could see her eyelashes blinking. There was a zigzag row of freckles across her nose like a railroad route on a map. I saw the shiny wet of tears on her crazy little girl's face.

"I don't want to stay here any more," she said. "Why did we come here anyway?"

"Because it was closed and I had the key."

She pushed the blanket down to her waist. The nudge of her breasts was like walnuts under her sweater. She had the tight, stubborn-child look on her mouth.

Because, I was thinking, she's got nothing left over for anyone else. And I wouldn't have either in her shoes. At least I was born legal and proper with all the due documentation and isn't that one hell of an advantage?

"...don't need you any more," she was saying. "I know where to go, just walk down the road to Nicky's and call up and they'll take me to Green Acres."

If I could tell her, I thought, but in the first place, she wouldn't believe me and in the second place, if it shouldn't work out...

"Because Mr. Prince said I could go there."

The thing in my shoulder was screaming at me.

"Marianne, listen—we'll go in a few minutes. I have to wait a little longer. Then I'll have to have a little help to get back to the car and we'll go. We'll get something to eat—"

She went to the door.

"Wait—"

She waited, poised at the door, the little lines hard around her mouth.

"What?" she said.

"Don't go to Nicky's. Go to the gas station on the corner. Call Lieutenant Sharp, a policeman. Tell him who you are and tell him where I am—"

"Why should I?"

"For yourself; just for yourself—"

"I don't know—"

She went out quickly. The door slammed shut.

I was sweating ice water. When the shaking started, I pulled the blanket around my neck and rolled with it. It was the acme of chills and before it was over, the couch was shaking in rhythm. When it subsided, I forced myself onto my good elbow, swung my feet over the edge and sat up. The room took a couple of spins, then straightened itself out. The drag of my arm was too much for the wound and I slid my forearm onto my lap and wadded the blanket under it for support.

When I got to my feet, the floor tilted and I kicked it back to level. Holding my elbow with my good hand, I went into the bedroom. Somebody had come in and cleaned it up. There was no sign that anything unusual had happened.

The wardrobe in the dressing alcove stood open and I felt among the odds and ends of abandoned summer clothing. A woman's silk scarf hung from a hook. In order to knot it, I had to let my arm hang free. I got it over my head and worked my left arm into it and it made a satisfactory sling. The fabric was soft on the back of my neck. I wondered whose it had been—Marianne's, Connie's, Karen's...

I propped myself against the wall. After a while I could lock my joints at will and it was time to go. There was no point in trying to score a beat on Marianne. At a reasonable pace, it would take her no more than fifteen minutes to walk to Pine Lake Road. Another three or four minutes, she would either be with Nicky, or on the highway. If she was lucky, she would get a ride with some disinterested person. If she was unlucky—

She had been born unlucky.

The cold, fresh air was bracing after the close interior, but as I looked down the lonely road, I wondered what had made me leave the car a quarter of a mile away. Anybody on the prowl, if they had got as far as the Bowman cottage, would have come on in, car or no. But at the time it had seemed like a good idea and I hadn't been in pain yet and you do funny things.

It was brutal going on the dark road, stumbling in the chuck holes. Within sight of the borrowed car drop, I stopped to rest. My mouth was dry and cottony. The cold air in my nostrils had the odor of blood.

The garage door groaned, rising, and clattered at the top when the springs recoiled. I felt my way along the left side of the car, got the door open and pushed myself onto the seat. After a pause for breath, I could reach across to pull the door to. I got the thing started and the fights on and turned on the heater, but the chill came on.

I clenched my teeth and rode it out, cursing the heater, the car, the dealer who had sold it to me and the company that had made it. It helped. None of them would ever hit back. All they would do would be to sell me another car.

When the chill passed, I found a rag in the glove compartment and wiped my face. The rag was gritty with oil. I rolled the window down and had myself a spit against the garage wall. Then I rolled the window up, backed out and onto the road.

The simple act of driving the car—admittedly primitive in design and with a useless heater—gave me new confidence. If I could manage this, who could tell to what heights I might rise with application and perseverance?

I drove slowly, avoiding most of the holes. With my left elbow propped on the arm rest, snug against the seat padding, I rode in relative comfort and there was nothing to the rest of it. One thing you had to say for the modern automobile, once you got it started and warmed up, it would keep rolling.

* * * *

As the trees thinned on both sides, I began to see the reflected lights of traffic on the highway. I couldn't see much else.

But I saw Marianne.

She was fifty yards ahead, walking toward me on the left side of the road, far out on the shoulder. She moved with that odd little plodding stride, hugging her arms, stumbling frequently, her little chin stuck out in front, her feet slapping flatly on the gravel.

I stopped and rolled my window down. She didn't look at me till she came abreast of the car and I called to her. Then her head turned slowly till she was seeing me.

"Run into a road block?" I said.

She looked down and kicked at a pebble.

"No," she said. "I just decided to come back."

"I'm not there any more."

"So I see."

"Better get in here. It's warmer."

After a moment, she got her chin up again and walked around the front of the car, moving primly through the glare of the headlights. She sat close against the door, looking straight ahead.

"Why did you come back?" I asked.

She shrugged and looked out the window.

"Because—" she said, "if you were hurt—I wanted to see if you were all right."

I reached and found her hand in the dark. She held back for a moment, then squeezed my fingers shyly. Her hand was dry and cold.

"You're a big girl now," I said. "All of a sudden, you're a big girl. I think they'll be proud of you at Green Acres."

"Is that where we're going?"

"First thing in the morning."

I got the car rolling. Pretty soon she said, "I don't know if I want to go there."

"It will be different at first, but you'll like it after a while."

"I don't know—" she said.

Pretty soon she slid closer and put her head on my shoulder. I got onto the highway, headed for Chicago, and within three miles, she had fallen asleep. She slept through a brief stop at an outlying drugstore and through a radio news report to the effect that I, a private detective, was wanted for questioning in connection with the disappearance of young woman named Marianne McLeod. Chicago police had been alerted, on the theory that I might head for home. I switched the thing off and made sure Marianne was asleep. She was. She was quite a sleeper. It could just be that she was one of the greatest sleepers in the history of Steel City, in all the ways anyone cared to mention.

CHAPTER TWENTY-FOUR

It was just after midnight when I found a place to park in an unlimited time zone in the neighborhood of the Second National Bank, Branch 42. I had a spare sports jacket in the car. It was no contribution to male fashion, but it didn't have a bloodstained hole in the shoulder and I got into it without too much difficulty. I would miss the sling, but found that by keeping my left hand in my pocket I could minimize the drag. My vision was off by now and I tripped a couple of times getting the suit box and my bag to the curb.

"Why all the stuff?" she said.

"New clothes for you," I said. "You wouldn't want them stolen, would you?"

I never felt that I could explain much in advance to her. She was automatically against anything she heard for the first time. I wasn't up to argument.

She picked up the box and I took the bag and we started down the street. Her feet slapped lightly on the cement. We came to an all-night cafeteria and I stopped her.

"Still hungry?" I asked.

She looked wistfully at the steamed window and nodded. As we entered, with typical negligence, she let the glass door swing back on me. I managed to twist and catch it with my good shoulder. The odor of hot food sent my stomach into a spin.

They had a good assortment of clean-looking entrees and I tried to suggest one of them, but she shrugged me off.

"A hot dog," she said.

"A glass of milk?"

She shook her head and I gave up. The idea of solid food was repulsive. I ordered a cup of coffee and four cartons of buttermilk, paid the tab and followed her to a white enamel table toward the front.

We didn't talk at first. Marianne wolfed the hot dog and I gave her money to get another. She held the change tightly in her clenched fist all the way and gave it up reluctantly at the cash register.

The buttermilk helped the stomach-settling department and the coffee sparked my energy to the point where I could undertake a mundane chore.

"One of the things you'll learn in your new home," I said, "is how and what to eat."

She stared at me with a mouthful of hot dog.

"What's wrong with this?" she said.

"That's all you've eaten since I met you. Hot dogs and that other stuff."

"Well," she looked down at my empty cartons. "Look who's talking. What kind of food is that?"

"I have special reasons," I said. "I also eat steak, seafood and fowl, all colors of vegetables, milk and fruit juice."

She finished the hot dog, wiped her mouth with exaggerated daintiness and cocked her head absurdly.

"So what?" she said.

"Hot dogs are all right once in a while. The stuff you're drinking will rot your teeth and louse up your blood count."

"At the Farm we had hot dogs almost every day. Hot dogs and beans. And there was a soft-drink machine, if you had the money. I didn't like the beans, they make you swell up—"

"That's quite a recommendation, that Farm cuisine."

"Farm what—? Well, I mean they have to take care of our health, don't they? They're interested in our health!"

"No, they aren't. They're interested in saving money. If they would serve a well-balanced diet, the taxpayers' association would overturn the government."

"At Thanksgiving and Christmas we had roast turkey with mashed potatoes and gravy."

"All right," I said, "I guess the taxpayers' association overlooked those two days. You want another hot dog?"

"No, I had enough."

"No, *thank* you," I said.

"Try it once."

"What?"

"Never mind. Let's go."

Going out, I was watchful, but this time she remembered and held the door carefully till I had cleared it. As we resumed our walk, she slipped her free hand into my coat pocket and kept it there all the way to the hotel.

While I signed in with a name like Jones or Smith or Brown, paying in advance, Marianne browsed through the comic book section of the magazine rack. I bought six of them for her and the tired, myopic clerk didn't even blink. The only time he got his chin off his chest was when he pointed out the elevator, and we carried our own stuff up to the room. It had a double bed, a dresser with a wide, walnut-framed mirror, an overstuffed chair and a picture on the wall depicting an assault on a medieval castle. Everything was clean enough.

Marianne took one look at the bed and flopped on her back, kicking off her sandals. Her skirt hiked up beyond the rolled tops of her stockings. She held the comic books like a spread deck of cards, making a selection.

I found a bottle of aspirin in my bag and went into the bathroom. I took four of the aspirin and sat down for a while to ride out a wave of nausea. In the room, Marianne was curled up with the adventures of Tanya the Tiger Woman and the Cannibal Pygmies.

"I have to go out for a while," I said.

"Okay," she said.

I stalled some, rattling the doorknob, but it was too far back to me from deep in the African veldt.

* * * *

My car, parked at the lonely curb, was a friendly point of reference. I ran my hand along the polished metal of the sill and apologized for the bad thoughts I had held earlier. I got in and sat for a while on the familiar seat. Pretty soon I took my gun from the glove compartment and dropped it into my coat pocket on the good side. It wasn't friendly like the car, but it served as ballast, a counterweight against my fist in the other pocket. I might have sat there the rest of the night, but dizziness drove me to my feet and I walked the block and a half and climbed the necessary stairs.

CHAPTER TWENTY-FIVE

Light laced the bottom edge of her door like a fine mist. Reaching for the knocker, my fingernails scraped the panel. The door swung wide and she moved in the lamplight like something in flight, trailing silk and the fragrance of lilies. I felt myself go white as she came against me, her bare arms pressing my neck. I held her to keep myself from falling. Her mouth was at my face.

"Darling, I was so worried. I heard the news—" Then suddenly she knew. Under the sheer gown her body stiffened, pushed away. When I got inside and found the light switch, she was streaking for the telephone. I took the thing from her hand before she could dial. She backed off and her eyes were winter; deep-set and cobalt blue under the jutting brow.

"You—" she said.

No phony frumpiness now. No glasses. Her hair framed her face softly. There was color in it, deep red on her lips. She wore a diaphanous negligee and mules on her bare feet.

"If you don't mind," I said, "we'll sit down."

"I'll kill you," she said. "I swear, if you give me one second, I'll kill you."

Her generous breasts, freed from restraint, rose and fell deeply.

"I'm sorry," I said. "Please sit down."

"Get out."

I backed to the wall and leaned there beside the telephone. Mrs. Carmichael held her ground. It was hurting me to breathe. Talking would be a bad chore—and for other reasons.

"I imagine it's a relief to let yourself go," I said, "now that you're free. Now that sister Connie is dead."

Nothing changed in her face. She just waited for that opening, the chance to kill me.

"The similarity in initials wouldn't prove anything," I said. "Like a pay-off to George Carmichael by C for Connie W for Waters. And Lilian W for Waters Carmichael. Could be coincidence. But other things kept cropping up—dates, associations, until coincidence was working overtime and finally broke down."

"You're crazy," she said quietly.

"Take the dates. You married George Carmichael in Las Vegas on December 19, 1952. Two days later, Anita McLeod died, on December 21. On December 22, you rented a safe deposit box at your own bank in the name of Lilian W. Carmichael."

Something went wrong in my head. I pushed the telephone off the stand and sat on it. Her hand went to her throat.

"I warn you," she said, "I'll find a way—"

"We know that Connie Waters shared a safe deposit box with Anita McLeod. And we know that less than a week ago, you canceled the Lilian Carmichael box, on the morning of the first banking day after Connie died. The only conclusion that adds up is that you required a box under some name other than Waters for a specific period of time between the deaths of Anita McLeod and Connie Traven."

I felt the stand buckle under me and got on my feet in time. Nothing splintered. The stand was all right; it had been me buckling. She was watching me with those eyes and they had changed. They were less opaque. They hurt. Also, they were a little crafty as she took in for the first time that I hurt too.

"I wish you'd sit down," I said. "You're distracting me. With that light behind you—"

She turned abruptly, went to the davenport and sat down primly. I eased myself into the wing chair, facing her.

"What do you want?" she said.

"Nothing much—confirmation, if you can see your way clear. Or stop me if I'm wrong. A respectable bank clerk with seniority can't just go out and change her name without some reason. It would look funny. So this marriage and divorce—attorney fees, one dollar. An attorney doesn't work for nothing. It's not ethical, and Pete Bowman was an ethical man. But he might stretch a point for a close friend. I found no evidence that he was a close friend of yours, but he was a close friend of Connie's."

Her hand caressed the seat beside her, moving stiffly over the time-smoothed nap. Her nails were scarlet. At night she would paint them and every morning she would take it off and go neutral to work.

"You could make it easier," I said. "Maybe I wouldn't have to throw up everything I know. Some of it we could let die."

Her hand moved continually on the cushion in random arcs, away and back, half around and back again.

"Your sister had the principles of a jackal," I said. "As with many human jackals, she found ways to make decent people do her dirty work. The way she used with Pete Bowman is the oldest in the world. On Anita McLeod and her daughter she used the sweetness and light technique. Then there was you."

"What about me?" she prompted. "Tell me more."

"You were her sister and knew what she was. Her very existence was a threat to your respectability and security. If you denounced her, things would come to light and you couldn't have known how it would turn out. Anyway, all she wanted was for you to get that name changed, to rent a safe deposit box and, from time to time, take the contents of her box and transfer it to yours, or vice versa, on request. A telephone call and the thing was done in five minutes."

Her hand had stopped caressing the cushions. The blue eyes peered at me.

"So you went along out of fear and helplessness. Later there were other reasons, when you found out how many people could be hurt if Connie should blow her stack."

She shifted, her spine went rigid.

"Because there was somebody breathing down Connie's neck who really meant business. It must have been quite a moment for Ward Prince when he found you—"

"No!"

Winter was gone from her eyes now. They were hot and furious.

"But look," I said, "if I could figure it out from a few random notes, a homemade timetable, some routine snooping with most of the people involved dead—think how easily Prince could get onto her with the resources he had—"

"Shut up!" she said, with the cat sound now. She was shaking under the gown. "It wasn't for that. He loves me!"

The conviction was deep as memory.

"I'm sure he does," I said, "so can we let it go at that? If I may use your phone—"

We started up at the same time. I was sluggish. Her hand snaked out from behind the cushion and she lunged at my chair. There was an eight-inch brass letter opener in her hand.

But I had guessed wrong earlier. She was incapable of killing me, or anyone. She managed to stumble. I reached for her arm and she fell into my lap. The knife made a dull sound on the carpet. She lay on my thighs, her knees on the floor, sobbing. It must have hurt badly.

"Listen," I said, "the world isn't ending. The Internal Revenue beef can be squared—the cash can be discovered, the tax paid—"

Her face lifted, tear-streaked and shocked.

"Internal—cash—there was no money involved in that thing with Connie!"

I stared at her. It took me a minute or so to catch on. I put my hands on her shoulders lightly.

"You didn't know about the money," I said. "I never thought of that. All you knew about was the blackmail stuff, a few dirty pictures. If it had been a matter of money, you could have refused her, let her take her own chances. But that other put you in a panic. That was the real threat, a handful of shame."

She shook herself free of my hands and pushed to her feet.

"Don't touch me," she said. "I'm somebody else's girl."

"I believe you good."

There was the sound of a key in the lock. I braced myself in the chair, decided against getting up. I put my hand in my pocket and felt the crude bulge of the gun. The door opened and Prince came in. He took in the room at a glance, closed the door quietly and stood, very big, watching.

"I seem to find you everywhere," he said.

"He knows," Lilian said dully.

Prince raised his hand and passed it slowly across the back of his neck. His eyes were remote and thoughtful. He came around the sofa, ignoring me, and put his arm around Lilian. They kissed. He led her to the bedroom door and opened it for her.

"Lie down and rest," he said. "I'll be right here."

She kissed him quickly and went into the bedroom. I had the gun half out of my pocket when he turned to come back, but his hands were empty and clean. I had noticed that about him, his immaculate hands, since the first time I had laid eyes on him. He came to the sofa and sat where she had been sitting.

"How much do you know, Mac?" he asked. "A whole lot, or just little pieces?"

"Quite a lot," I said. "No man knows everything."

"Tell me," he said.

"I know that Connie Traven had the secret of Green Acres. I know she was blackmailing Karen Bowman on the side on the basis of the stuff she had on Pete. She may have been getting some from you, too, if she had the guts. Guts run in her family. Her sister just tried to kill me with a letter opener."

He glanced at the closed bedroom door.

"Go on," he said.

"I don't like to go on. I don't like to break up a thing like you have with Mrs. Carmichael. I don't like having to pull people's insides out and hold them up to their own eyes. If I do it now, do you know why?"

It took time, but finally he nodded.

"I might," he said.

"You're a remarkable fellow and I wish we had met a long time ago. When I think of that temple you built at Green Acres, single-handed, out of a few acres of space and a doubtful legend, I can hardly believe it, even though I've seen it. Of course, you made the one mistake, and, like the mistakes of big men, it was a beaut. Wasn't it?"

His face was stiff, impassive. He did the business with his hand on his neck and then he nodded once more.

"I guess you know a lot," he said.

"More than I need. I don't want to destroy the temple. I think it ought to stand."

He smiled and shook his head.

"I'm not sure enough of you. I can't just ride along on your bluff. If you don't mind, you're somewhat remarkable yourself."

I wiped my face hard with my hands and found him again. He hadn't moved.

"All right," I said, "now we've got the amenities out of the way, tell me something. What would it be worth to you to get Nicky Royal out of your hair?"

All he did was to shift from one buttock to the other, recross his legs and push himself back against the cushions. It was enough.

"He's been in there a long time, hasn't he?" I said. "A twisted case of hero worship. A slave gets to be a nuisance, especially when he does his own thinking. Like finding out about—this—here—so when Deacon Roberts came around, Nicky figured out that he was trying to get something on you. So Roberts had to go. It doesn't matter that all the Deacon really wanted was Anita McLeod's money. He's just as dead."

"You're guessing," Prince said.

"Come on. The Deacon told us—some 'punk,' he said, 'young, dark, with a voice.' Nothing? Half a million punks in town. But Nicky tried to do the same thing to me when I grabbed Marianne out of that conference you set up. And I knew he was working for you."

"How did you know?"

"Because you're never too old to learn and an old friend taught me what to do with a wrist watch, which is to look at it from time to time. He gave me a good lesson just the other night. Three minutes after the Deacon died, we were here in this apartment. Mrs. Carmichael knew Roberts was dead. Before we left, Donovan checked on the bedroom. Someone was there; he didn't tell me who. It had to be either someone he trusted or someone he feared. The second alternative was ridiculous, so it was someone he trusted, at least provisionally. A few minutes later we were at the precinct station. We learned they'd had a call from you about the Deacon. When they tried to call you back at Green Acres, you weren't there. Donovan looked at his watch. He still couldn't come right out and tell me it had been you here in the bedroom. But he could give me the equipment with which to figure it out."

Prince cleared his throat lightly.

"And you did," he said.

"After a while. It worked out all right. Donovan would go a long way with a man of your reputation. I don't know exactly how you got through to him without a conversation that I could have overheard—"

"That was simple enough," he cut in. "Your man Donovan isn't one to sound off on the spur of the moment. I had my ID out and a note written in large letters by the time he came into the bedroom. The note was a promise to meet him at headquarters with a full explanation. It satisfied him, and I did meet him."

He smiled a little dryly. "I couldn't know you were both so time conscious."

"Well, anyway that's how it was done. When you told me at Green Acres that a cab driver had mentioned taking Marianne out to the Bowman cottage, I looked at my watch. The cabbie couldn't have told the police, because they didn't know anything themselves until half an hour earlier. It wasn't in the papers. No reason for Charlie to mention it till something happened. But he would tell Nicky, if Nicky asked him, and Nicky would get it back to you."

"Aren't you giving Nicky a lot of credit? At that hour of the morning, assiduously making his rounds—"

"If he knew that, the night before, Pete Bowman had visited Marianne—yes." I looked into his eyes. "He wouldn't have to see the visit with his own eyes. He could have been told. The same way he was told to keep an eye on the Traven apartment and did his job so well, he went all the way to Chicago on Traven's tail. Tipping the cops was something that never would have occurred to Nicky, unless he was told to do it. So he was told. And Sergeant Downs killed Traven, with an innocent, unwitting assist by Pete Bowman."

His eyes had gone distant on me. There was something new around his mouth.

"That relief you felt when Connie Traven was dead didn't last long, did it?" I said. "Didn't you get a little scared when the killing kept going on? With Nicky all over the place?"

He got up then and took a turn around the sofa.

"I tried every way to keep Nicky in bounds," he said. "I had to know where the Deacon was going. I couldn't tail him officially. It had to be Nicky."

"How long had Nicky known about—this?" I couldn't think of a name I wanted to give it.

"Lilian and me? As far as I know, never before."

"He must have. He was your private, self-appointed bodyguard and champion."

"I didn't know, until that night."

"Well, by now you know—something will have to be done about Nicky."

"Like what?"

"Suppose we put it up to Nicky right now."

He showed surprise for the first time.

"Mac, there's a limit. You're not psychic—"

"Three to one," I said, "he's out there in the hall right now." There had been nothing psychic about it. There had just been a logical conclusion based on experience. Prince didn't want to believe it, but he had to find out. He opened the door and the kid was there all right, a little sheepish, mumbling,

"Mr. Prince—I thought you might need something—"

Prince's hand clenched behind his head, but his voice was calm. "Come in, Nicky."

He came in, wary, but still swaggering, twitching here and there.

"Caught up with him, huh?" he said to Prince.

"Not exactly," Prince said.

Nicky looked around slyly and backed toward the door.

"If the cops are coming, you won't need me—" Prince pushed the door to. Nicky blinked at him.

"The police aren't coming right away," Prince said.

Nicky's eyes swiveled to me.

"I don't get it," he said. "They're looking for this peeper for hours! Here he is—" The strength was oozing out of me like sap from a tree. I pushed up with my good arm and it wasn't too bad after I got on my feet.

"I'll do it," I said to Prince. "Nicky, you killed Deacon Roberts."

"You're nuts," he said.

He quit looking at me and concentrated on Prince.

"You going to let him stand there—"

"The Deacon talked before he died," I said. "An amateur, he called you. He gave us a description."

"No!"

"Yeah, Nicky. And you were on your own. Mr. Prince didn't tell you to kill the Deacon, did he?"

He moved out from Prince and pivoted, giving himself room. There was a bruise on his face where I had hit him on his own front porch.

"Can he prove it?" he asked Prince.

"I think he can, Nicky," Prince said.

He shot that left cuff of his.

"Well, you're not going to let him get away with it! Look, he's got a hole in him! We can take him—"

Prince shook his head.

"No, Nicky."

Nicky backed off with his arms out, his torso twisted. He looked like a spider.

"Then I'll take him myself. What's he? Nothing! Goddamn it, nothing!"

I went for the gun and it caught on the flap of my pocket. Wrenching at it, I went off balance and fell against the chair, sprawling. He had the knife out in front. He went into that little dance step of his, swinging toward me, covering ground fast. There were only six feet between us and his arm was thirty inches long. The gun was down between the chair arm and the seat with my own weight on it.

Desperate to free it, I threw myself onto my bad shoulder. In a blur, I saw Prince move, swing his big hand in a sweeping curve. I knew what a wallop it carried. There was a thick slapping sound. Nicky went back and half around before he hit the wall between the telephone stand and the bedroom door. By then I was on my feet with the gun out and nothing on which to use it.

Nicky was on his knees, shaking his head, still holding the knife.

"But, Mr. Prince—" he said.

"Damn you, Nicky, I should have done that years ago, when you first came hanging around. There's no room on my back for you. Can't you understand that? Wherever you go from here, you'll have to take your mother's little secret with you."

Slowly Nicky got to his feet, hugging the wall for support.

"My mother's what? You crazy or something?"

"Don't give me that now," Prince said wearily. "Your mother must have told you—"

"My mother never told me nothing! Since I was a little kid, my mother couldn't talk! Had a stroke. My aunt took care of her. Some aunt. She got a check every month for a hundred bucks. She spent twenty-five of it on me and my mother and put the rest in her pocket. She didn't ask questions. When my mother died and I lit out, I knew your name. I read about you in the paper. That's all. When I got in that rap, you gave me a break—I hung around. Why not? So the hell with it. But don't blame it on my mother!"

He stood still against the wall. He looked at me.

"All right, big man," he said. "What're you going to do?"

The bedroom door opened and Lilian came into the room. She still wore the filmy robe, but was in her bare feet. They looked small and virginal on the old carpet. She looked searchingly at Prince and edged toward him, skirting Nicky warily. His eyes slanted to her and held on. Prince froze where he stood. I kept my voice low.

"Drop the knife, Nicky."

But Nicky knew a break when he saw one. She was within arm's reach and no marksmanship medal in the world is license to cut it that fine. He had her between us in a watch tick's time, his left arm around her waist from behind. She went white, but didn't try to fight him. Prince's hands were helpless fists, half raised.

"Don't be a fool, Nicky," he said.

He pushed backward through the swinging kitchen door, pulling her with him. I took two steps toward them and he put the knife to her throat. The door caught, failed to swing to. He held onto her long enough to nudge the back screen open. Then he let go and plunged out of sight. I heard his feet slapping the wooden steps.

Prince and I met at the kitchen door.

"Give it to me," he said hoarsely, reaching for the gun.

"Let him go for now," I said. "It will give me a break too."

He stared at me.

"I have to finish it," I said. "You must know that."

He left me and went to Lilian. She was standing with her hands at her temples, her eyes closed. I watched her red-tipped fingers crawl over his back. I went into the living room and picked up the phone, replaced it on the stand and stood around, waiting.

"I'll make some coffee," I heard Lilian say.

The kitchen door swung to and Prince came into the room. His head was shaking slowly. He had the far-off look that comes in a big man's eyes when he begins to crumble.

"He never knew," he said. "All that time, he knew nothing. And I let him ride me."

"I have to make a call," I said.

He seemed startled to see me.

"Your friend Donovan?" he said.

"If I'm lucky."

I took the thing off the hook and he said, "Wait."

I hung up.

"Now?" I said.

He nodded. He sat on the sofa, rubbing his face with his hands and pretty soon he began to talk.

CHAPTER TWENTY-SIX

It took about five minutes. It seemed strange that it should take such a short time.

"Connie Traven was collecting from me every month for more than three years. Three hundred, then four, then five. I've been well paid at Green Acres and I'd saved some. She was eating it up. I didn't know she was getting it from Karen too. I was helpless. Eliminating her would still leave Nicky. I couldn't kill everyone in sight."

"What did she have concrete?" I cut in. "Or was it just hearsay from Anita McLeod?"

He shook his head ruefully.

"An affidavit, signed by Anita McLeod. At my instance."

"In the safe deposit box?"

He nodded.

"That bothers me," I said. "Why couldn't you and Lilian have emptied that box and let Connie sing for her supper?"

"Because she would have sung. Loud and clear."

"I didn't mean to interrupt," I said. "When did you decide to kill her?"

"The day it happened. When I found out she'd been blackmailing Karen too. It was my regular pay-off day, but not Karen's. The woman had rigged a system, a thing in the window to show the coast was clear. No husband, no nosy neighbor. I'd go up and make the pay-off and get out.

"That day I went up and made the pay-off as usual. As I was leaving, she raised the ante on me. 'Next time, six hundred,' she said. I think that's what started it. I was hot all over. When I got downstairs my hands were shaking. Then I ran into Karen, just entering the building."

"And you knew?"

"One look and I knew. I had known about Pete and Connie and I knew what she was doing to me. I just had never put the things together. I put it up to Karen and she finally broke down and told me. That's all it took. I went back upstairs and she was in the bedroom with that strongbox. I saw the key hanging on her necklace. When I asked for the stuff on Pete, she just laughed. I grabbed for the key and she stumbled near the bed. I had hold of the neck chain and I guess I knew what it could do.

"I held her face down on the bed and strangled her. It didn't take long. By the time she got rid of the strongbox, she was too far gone to fight.

"I found the evidence on Pete, checked through the other stuff, cleaned up what I had touched and got out. Karen was waiting in her car—" He kept slipping in and out of focus. I got on my feet and propped myself against the wall again. I had the feeling you get when you're stuffed and someone keeps forcing food on you and you keep eating—all the wrong things—out of inertia or weariness. All of it seemed far-off and meaningless and the only important thing left in the whole dismal story was Marianne and even she might not be worth it. But he kept on with it…"

"Karen and I went back to Green Acres. I kept in touch with the police calls, sent her home about eight in the evening—"

"With the blackmail evidence?"

"Yes. I wanted to destroy it, but she wanted Pete to have proof he was off the hook."

"All right. What about Traven?"

"When they hadn't discovered Connie by nine o'clock, I sent Nicky to keep his eye on things. He saw Traven come home and run out. He followed him. When I got the police call on it, I didn't know anything about Traven or the quarrel. Nicky telephoned from Chicago and I told him to keep in touch. When I found out what a case the police had on Traven, I couldn't believe it. I knew it would break down, but in the meantime Traven would be safer in custody. I didn't figure on Sergeant Downs."

"Are you telling me that Sergeant Downs was not in your pocket?"

"Well, partially; not to that extent."

"And that you wouldn't have let Traven take the rap if it had come to that?"

"Of course."

"I'm glad to hear it."

Lilian came in with coffee and cups on a tray. She set it on an end table within reach of Prince, but let me walk over and get my own. She wouldn't look at me. She sat beside him on the sofa with her hands folded on her knees.

"What about Pete Bowman?" I asked.

"It was an accident, as you guessed. Except that I was there. I couldn't have prevented it. He had the gun between his knees and his little can of oil and a rag. He was fooling with it while we talked."

"How did you happen to be there?"

"He had called me, said he was at the cottage and had to see me at once. He'd been working on the Traven thing on his own. Having been in on Lilian's divorce, he had something to go on and when he was sober, Pete Bowman was no fool."

"How far had he got?"

"Pretty far. He knew most of it."

"About Marianne?"

"Yes. He put it up to me. His whole aim was to clear Traven. But Traven was dead, and I think, for Karen's sake and her father's and the whole complex of what Green Acres stood for, he'd have called it off—on one condition."

"That something be done about Marianne."

"Yes."

"And that's what you were trying to do when I found her with Nicky—"

"I guess I should have known you well enough by then," he said.

"I made a deathbed promise," I said.

They sat, stiffly silent, side by side. I lifted the phone and Lilian's hand moved to his thigh and lay on it lightly. He covered it with his own.

I dialed Chicago headquarters. The man in Homicide was unknown to me, so I could assume, as far as voices were concerned, it worked both ways.

"I've got a lead for Lieutenant Donovan," I said, "in the Deacon Roberts rubout."

"Come on with it," he said. "We'll follow through."

"Just the Lieutenant. Alone. In the lobby of the Greene Hotel." I gave him the address.

"Hold on a minute—"

"Just get the word to the Lieutenant," I said.

I hung up. They were watching me from the sofa. Lilian's blue eyes met mine and lingered, remote and cold for the rest of our lives. I had done her no service.

"Do you want me to go with you now?" Prince asked.

I shook my head. "I'll take the same chance Donovan did. You know the way to headquarters. Being a type who's full of advice, I'll throw some your way: don't tell anybody anything except on the advice of an attorney."

I started out and he said, "As you put it earlier, I wish we had met a long time ago."

I made my way carefully down the endless stairs.

No, you don't, I thought. You wish you had never heard of me in your life and you might have been man enough to admit it.

CHAPTER TWENTY-SEVEN

Marianne, fully dressed, had dozed off in a litter of comic books. She yawned and sat up while I shrugged out of my coat, got my shoes and socks off and launched the delicate business of removing my bloodstained shirt. She caught me at it and looked away quickly, repelled.

I had the bag open between my feet and I hauled out the paper sack from the drugstore and opened a box of sterile gauze pads.

"What's that?" she said.

"We're going to play a little game," I said. "Doctor and patient."

She looked at me with suspicion.

"Don't worry," I said. "I'll play both parts."

"Can I open the things you got me now?" she asked.

"By all means. You'll have a little privacy while I wash up."

With my shirt hanging raggedly from my shoulder I headed for the bathroom.

"What's the difference?" she said. "You already saw that picture of me."

I went on in and closed the door. The shirt came away more readily than I had a right to expect, but it took some time to sponge off the mess. He had torn it badly, jerking the knife clear. If I could have done it quickly, it would have saved wear and tear on my nerves, but I couldn't risk starting another flow that I might be unable to stop. I studied the wound and it didn't look too dangerous, but underneath the superficial flesh, the greedy bugs would be working.

I cleaned myself elsewhere awkwardly, rinsed out the bloodstained bowl and went back to the bed. It was well occupied. Marianne had laid out her entire wardrobe, an assortment of gaily packaged feminine items, ranged in rows, carefully squared and spaced. There were three pairs of hose, four panties, two blouses, a wrinkled peasant skirt, spread fanwise, the green and blue dresses and two nightgowns, one blue and one pink, draped over the foot of the bed. She was standing off, squinting at them.

"I don't know whether to wear the blue one or the pink one," she said.

"Well," I said, "I hate to disturb the layout, but I have to get in that bed. Maybe you could wear all of them at once."

"Don't be silly," she said.

I opened the bed and she put the things back in the bag, item by item, carefully. The two nightgowns she left out.

I propped up a pillow, got the package of first aid supplies within reach and climbed in. It seemed a waste of valuable energy to take off my pants, so I left them on. The bed was firm and smooth and I settled onto it gratefully. Stretched out as I was, with my shoulders raised against the headboard, I felt myself slipping and worked to get back, searching the room for Marianne.

She had got her shoes and stockings off and was walking away from them. Heedlessly she skinned out of her sweater, unzipped her skirt and let it lie. She pulled her slip over her head, pushed her panties to her ankles and kicked them away. Then she went to the dresser and looked at herself in the square mirror. I was looking for the iodine bottle and the rubber syringe when she said, "Boy, there's a real nothing!"

She was trying to cup her breasts with her hands. It was a vain effort. There just wasn't enough basic material.

"What'll I do?" she wailed.

"Don't worry about it. Eat good food, exercise, be happy. A few years, you'll get married, have babies—everything will work out fine."

"There are things a girl can do about it," she said. "There was a girl at the Farm, a stripper—"

"Marianne, listen. The sooner you forget the girls on that Farm, the better."

"Well she knew what she was talking about, didn't she? A stripper like that—"

"You want to be a stripper?"

"She used to make five hundred dollars a week. A week!"

"What was she doing at the Farm?"

She looked away.

"I don't know—she was a junkie—" She scowled darkly. "You're getting to be like that parole officer. Everything I say, you give me a lecture."

"It's about all I'm up to."

She came to the foot of the bed and studied the two nightgowns.

"I know I'm impossible to get along with," I said, "but wouldn't you like to take a bath first?"

I'd as well have invited her to leap into a volcano.

"I had a bath—"

"Yesterday already."

"But why?"

I couldn't stand the pace. "Because Shakespeare said cleanliness is next to godliness. Suit yourself."

I clamped the iodine bottle between my knees and screwed the cap loose. The fingers of my left hand were tingling dully and I couldn't afford to fool around with it. Marianne stood, the nightgown a disordered ruff around her neck. When she saw I wasn't paying attention, she pulled it off and stamped away to the bathroom. A minute later I heard water splashing in the tub. Pretty soon that stopped and I visualized her lying in the tub, dreaming up ways to get even with me.

A numbness had set in around the wound. I felt drowsy, but my head was clear and the atmosphere free of dancing lights. I sucked some iodine up into a rubber syringe and set it on the bedside table. I picked up my nearly useless left arm and got my fingers onto the smooth edge of the headboard. One thing you had to say for the old brass bedsteads—there was something for a man to hang onto.

I glared at the black telephone beside the syringe. The hand gripping the headboard was shaking, but it held on. I clamped my teeth, took a deep breath and squeezed off.

* * * *

The sequence of events in the next few minutes has never been straightened out for me. I remember the banging of the telephone when I pushed it off the stand. I heard men's voices, but that was really later. My first clear memory is of lying between the stand and the bed and a man's hands under me, rolling me back into position.

Somebody said, "Want me to call a doctor?"

"Don't call nobody!" the voice said gruffly. "Just go back to the desk and set there."

The voice came through, but slowly and I didn't really believe in it till I could get my eyes focused on him. I remember looking for Marianne and not finding her. The bathroom door was closed. I settled for Donovan, standing beside the bed.

"I said I'd meet you in the lobby," I said.

"Uh-huh," he said. "When? Next week?"

He looked around at Marianne's abandoned wraps and his nose wrinkled.

"Some double life," he said. "I never thought it of you."

"Now you know."

"She here with you? They want her."

"It's time somebody wanted her."

"About that tip you phoned in—the Deacon?"

"We have to deal," I said. "Break for break."

"Just go ahead and talk, Mac."

"Look, you pig-headed son-of-a-bitch, you did this to the Deacon and he was dying right before your eyes. You made him deal."

He grinned. He felt better now. I wasn't going to die on him. "You never could learn to cry, could you?" he said.

"Don't ever think it. A youngster named Nick Royal did it. Lives on Pine Lake Road, across the street from Green Acres. He did it on his own, nobody paid him, nobody nudged him."

"All right, go ahead."

"When you find him, he may run off some. Everybody around Steel City tries to get behind Ward Prince and Green Acres. Don't pay any attention to it."

"Don't tell me my business, kid, just the facts, like the man says." He hadn't called me kid for a long time. I guessed he had the right.

"He may still be in town," I said. "Just before I called in, he got away from me at Mrs. Lilian Carmichael's apartment."

He picked up the phone and dialed. His sharp eyes made a tour of my upper trunk.

"Sharp doors you run into," he said. "How long you had that?"

"Not long."

I heard him mumbling the stuff on Nick Royal to someone on the other end. There was a pause and he glanced down at me.

"Some poor wino," he said. "Holed up in a pad on the South Side. Better get the Steel City people on this kid."

He hung up and walked away, pausing here and there to nudge at one of Marianne's garments with his foot.

"I have to take you in," he said. "They're very hot for you and the girl."

"If they are, it's just a matter of pride."

"So," he said, "if you know where she is and want to turn her over, I think you can get out of it pretty clean."

"And if I don't?"

"Like I said, they're after you."

He did some more walking.

"Look," I said, "you touted me off on this thing. You were the one that took me along to see the Deacon. You pushed me!"

Then we couldn't quite face each other.

"I guess I did," he said.

"Well, what I got into was an atomic-type explosion with a delayed action fuse about twenty years long. It was the fall-out that did the damage. The fall-out killed Connie Traven and her husband and Pete Bowman and Deacon Roberts."

"Pretty fancy talk."

"Sorry. I'm just not sure whose side you have to be on."

"Neither am I. I'd hate to see you go up in this explosion just to make a name for yourself."

"What if it's to make a name for somebody else?"

He looked at me as if I were trying to trap him, which in a way I was.

"You have time for a story?" I said.

He didn't say, but he didn't walk out either. I told him Marianne's story in five sentences. When I finished, there was no way to know by his face whether he believed it or how he felt about it. "So to wrap it up," I said, "I have to go back there."

"You'll never make it. They'll have the roads blocked. I doubt if you could get to your own car before somebody will pick you up."

"There's a way, if you'll help. If you let them know that you picked us up and you will take us in—"

He shook his head stubbornly.

"If you had an innocent life hangin' on it. But don't be askin' me to go into another jurisdiction and throw my badge in the ashcan if all you want is to drop the roof on a lot of unsuspectin' people."

"You think that's all I want?"

"I know that Ward Prince was fixing it for the girl to go to Green Acres, and you stepped in—"

"All right. You mentioned an innocent life. What's the difference between dying clean in a hurry and being buried alive?"

"A lot of difference, as long as there's a chance to claw your way out. That's what life is."

I looked at his big face and the hard wisdom that showed so rarely. He was right from his own viewpoint. He was a public employee. He had to figure always that if an injustice couldn't be righted in a legal and orderly way, the cause itself was suspect. He would jump the traces from time to time, as when he had urged me into the Traven thing. But that had started with blatant, virtual murder about which he was officially powerless. The question of Marianne was quite a different matter.

He went to the door, picking his way among her discarded garments.

"Was there anything else you wanted to tell me?" he said. "Like what you were doing at Mrs. Carmichael's place?"

"No," I said.

"Well, you know the offer," he said. "You turn over the girl and work with the authorities instead of against 'em—"

"With Sergeant Downs?" I said. "With Ward Prince?"

"I'm just sayin' how you can get out fairly clean—"

"How clean?"

He shrugged massively.

"All right. I guess there's no talkin' to you. Want a doctor first?"

"No."

"I'll give you a little time to rest up. You don't look like a man that's goin' anywhere but in case you would consider it, don't try to leave the hotel."

He hung around for a few seconds, then I heard him going out. He didn't slam the door. All I could feel was drowsiness and the driving ache in my shoulder.

Marianne came out of the bathroom, pink-skinned, her hair wet around the edges. Her black mood was gone and she moved lithely around the room, clowning and dancing.

"Know what?" she said. "I fell asleep. Right in the tub."

My throat was too dry for comment. It felt clogged. I shook some aspirin tablets into my hand and wondered whether it would be worthwhile to get them down.

"Marianne," I called.

"What?"

"Would you please get me a glass of water?"

"Sure."

She went into the bathroom and got it and put it on the stand, then wandered away and began primping at her hair. I threw the aspirin into my mouth and washed it down, spilling quite a bit of the water in the process.

"You know what?" she said, watching me in the mirror.

"No, what?"

"You forgot to say thank you for the water."

So we were even. She had found a way.

"I'm sorry," I said. "It was rude of me."

After a moment I said, "Thank you."

"You're welcome."

I opened the package of gauze pads and a roll of adhesive tape. Her face twisted with revulsion and she went back to the bathroom.

"I just can't stand that. Tell me when you're through."

I fumbled at the dressing with my good hand, trying first to hold the tape with my left hand to tear it and, failing, trying with my teeth. This finally worked. I could get the tape onto the dressing all right, but then a piece of the tape stuck to the blanket and came away covered with lint. I swore in a steady blue stream. Lifting the pad to cover the wound, I plastered an end of tape to my chest and it stuck fast. I ripped it off and slammed it on the bed. Glancing up, I saw Marianne peeking around the edge of the bathroom door.

"Sorry," I said.

I got out a fresh pad and started again, working slowly and carefully, with concentration. I had one strip of tape neatly in place on the pad when I felt her close beside the bed. Her little face was tight and a muscle jumped beside her mouth. Her eyes were green slits. She took the pad from my hand.

"I'll do it," she said.

Her face looked more like an executioner's than that of an angel of mercy. But her fingers were quick and gentle and she placed the pad over the wound carefully, smoothed down the tape on one side, then applied the second strip and stuck it down.

"Is that all right?" she said.

"That's perfect. Thank you."

Braced on one hand over me, she breathed deeply and gradually her face relaxed. Her narrow, spare body was rigid. I put my hand on her face and she leaned down unexpectedly and kissed me, then jumped up, turning away.

"I'm freezing," she said.

She ran to the light switch, her tight little buttocks jiggling. Running back across the room in the dark, she was a wisp of wind-driven fog. I felt the bed dip. Then she was beside me, huddled close, shivering. Her fingers tangled in the hair on my chest and I could feel her chin in the hollow between my neck and shoulder.

"Mac—hold me. Hold me somewhere."

I found a place to hold her. One hand was sufficient. She was warm to the touch, despite the shivering. Pretty soon that stopped and she squirmed into a slender fullness along my ribs and thigh. "Mac—"

"What is it?"

"You said I'd get married—have babies."

"Sure. Why not?"

"I'm too small. I mean I don't think I could."

"Certainly you could. Have small ones."

I kept dropping off and waking to hear her still talking.

"You know who I always wanted to marry when I was a kid—after Connie got through with him I mean?"

"Not Pete Bowman?"

"Yeah. Even the other night when he came in the restaurant and I went outside with him for a minute and he had that big car—an Eldorado it was—"

I woke up.

"What?" I said.

"Nothing," she said. "It was silly."

I lay there, looking at the dark.

"If somebody comes along and I marry him," she said, "will he be like you?"

"God forbid."

"I'm not fooling. What will he be like?"

"I don't know. Some nice guy with a good job."

"Like you?"

"Not like me, honey. I'm a very nice guy all right, but I got a lousy job."

"I'm serious, Mac."

"All right."

"I wish he would be like you."

I turned my head a little and kissed her nose.

"When the time comes," I said, "we'll see. Go to sleep now."

It seemed like a very safe thing to say.

CHAPTER TWENTY-EIGHT

It was still dark in the room and a man was speaking to me in a low, urgent voice. Marianne lay heavily against me, sleeping soundly. I blinked awake and it was Donovan, crouched beside the bed.

"Time to go," he said.

I started rocking Marianne lightly with my arm.

"What's the hurry?" I said to him.

"I already give you three hours. It's six o'clock."

He straightened up and picked up the phone. I heard him dialing, then his voice, low and gruff.

"I picked up the guy and that girl the Steel City people are lookin' for," he said. "I'm bringin' 'em in... No, I don't need no help."

Marianne opened her eyes and shut them again.

"Wake up," I said. "We've got to go."

"Why?"

"Police," I said. "Cops."

She scrambled off the bed, caught sight of Donovan and froze, leaning, staring across at him.

"Who's he?" she whispered.

"An old friend," I said.

Donovan was trying not to look at her much.

"I'll help you get dressed," he said.

"I'll get dressed," I said. "You might throw some of those things in the bag."

He moved away and I pushed my legs off the bed and sat up, shaking my head to clear it. Marianne and Donovan were having a tug of war with a pair of panties.

"I have to wear them!" she said savagely.

Donovan growled. I saw her snatch up her clothes and run for the bathroom. I switched on the bedside lamp.

"At least you might have fed her," he said. "Put a little meat on her bones."

"The hell with it," I said. "Just make your pinch. It's no different from any other, only maybe a little spicier."

He turned away, looked around the room and snapped the bag shut. I had one arm in my coat and he helped with the other arm. Marianne was in the bathroom. I picked up the bag and knocked on the door. She came out, adjusting her skirt. Taking a new look at Donovan in the light, she stiffened and her face got that hard look again.

"Old friend!" she said. "He's a cop. I can tell."

"Come on," I said, "let's go—" She pulled away and her claws were all the way out.

"Listen, I didn't do anything. You tell him."

"He knows you didn't do anything," I said. "Try not to worry. You're on your way to Green Acres."

Donovan opened the door and held it, waiting. She looked at him some more and at me and around the room, a little wistfully, and she said, "Did you get all my stuff in the bag?"

"Yes," I said.

"Everything?"

"All of it."

"Okay," she said.

She marched past Donovan into the hall with her nose in the air. When I got out there, she was heading for the elevator.

"This way," Donovan said.

He turned and started off toward the back stairs. I tightened my grip on the bag and nodded to Marianne. She came along, hugging my arm with both hands. We caught up with Donovan at the top of the steps.

"How come the back way?" I asked.

He shrugged and started down.

"Don't want to draw a crowd," he said.

We made the perilous descent to the alley behind the hotel. Donovan's car was standing at the service entrance with the door open. He had turned down the volume on his radio and all you could hear on it was a brittle sputtering. He had no driver with him and there were no flashing blinkers.

Marianne hung back for a moment, but I urged her into the front seat and she slid on to it reluctantly. I put my bag in the back seat, got in beside her and closed the door. Donovan was under the wheel.

Marianne was shivering and I worked my arm up till I could lay it across her shoulder and made my fingers squeeze.

"Everything will be all right," I said. "We'll find a nice place and get some breakfast. If you want hot dogs, it's all right with me."

"You're crazy," she said. "Whoever eats hot dogs for breakfast?"

I hugged her and she put her face against my neck.

There's a role you can drop now, I thought, that Blue Island Pygmalion.

* * * *

Donovan drove fast away from the hotel, then slowed. My sense of direction was shot. It appeared that he had lost his way and I kept telling myself this was impossible. Coming down from the hotel, I had been very shaky. The pain had changed in intensity and I was edgy with it. But the cold morning air was bracing. The skies had cleared and it would be a nice day when the sun came up.

Donovan's car crawled over the deserted street. I blinked rapidly and saw my own car parked just ahead. Without warning, he pulled into the curb and stopped behind it. Marianne looked at him cautiously. He got out of the car, opened the back door and removed my bag. By then I had wit enough to open my own door and get Marianne out on the sidewalk. Donovan threw the bag into the back seat of my car. I went down there with Marianne and he held the door, waiting. She climbed in with a sigh and Donovan came around to the wheel side with me and helped me in.

"Can you drive?" he said.

"These modern cars, you don't have to drive. They took care of all that at the factory. It's just that sometimes the heaters—" He backed away from the window.

"So long, Lone Ranger," he said.

"So long, Lieutenant—" I fooled around getting it started. He looked both ways along the street and moved closer.

"There's an old saying," he said. "Keep moving. Don't stop. Don't look back."

I nodded and got away from the curb. When I looked back in the rear-view mirror, he was standing in the middle of the street, looking around.

CHAPTER TWENTY-NINE

It was, I thought, a very handsome little lake. In the early sun, the water was ice-smooth, with light and dark patches, reflections of the morning sky. Birds were chirping up a storm in the old trees.

You could live here a long time, I thought, without missing much.

A fly crawled through a hole in the screen and I made a pass at it and missed. The slight movement sent me reeling and I went out on the porch steps and sat down, watching the lake. After a while the kitchen door rattled and I heard the shuffle of Marianne's sandaled feet on the porch. She threw a spindly shadow on the wall beside the steps.

"We're right back where we started," she said.

"With a slight difference."

"Do I get to go there today?"

"This is the day."

"Is it all fixed?"

"Pretty soon now."

Her shadow deepened as the sun climbed. I watched the hard, stubborn line of her chin grow cleaner.

"By rights," she said, "I should be living there all the time. It was my mother's fault."

"It was?"

"She worked there when I was a little kid. For Mrs. Lloyd. Then they got sore about something and wouldn't let her stay there."

"Is that what your mother told you?"

"No. She never told me anything. Connie told me."

"What was she like, your mother?"

"She was all right. Kind of dumb."

"Connie was the smart one?"

"Sure. Connie knew how to take care of herself."

"Uh, huh."

"You sound like you don't believe me! Connie took good care of me."

"Like for instance, what did Connie do for you?"

"Everything! She got married on account of me. To that Traven."

"She did that for you?"

"Sure. Why would she marry him—such a square! When I got in that trouble and had to go to the Farm, she married him, so when I got out, I could stay with them. If she wasn't married, they might not let me live with her, on account of her having lived with us before, and the Deacon and all."

It figured. That marriage had clawed at the back of my mind. It hadn't ever made sense.

"But when you got out," I said, "you didn't go there to live with Connie."

"I was going to! She had to fix it with that husband of hers first."

I held my head in my hands for a while.

"She gave me money too," she said. "Whenever I needed it."

"How much, for instance?"

"Plenty. Once she gave me fifty dollars."

"Well."

"And she paid the lawyer for me when I was in trouble. It must have cost a hundred dollars."

"And the lawyer pleaded you guilty, talked it over with the judge and you got eighteen months. For a first offense. Shoplifting."

"What else could he do? I did it. It was something—I just saw it laying there and I didn't have any money, so I took it."

"I guess that's all he could do."

"Anyway, Connie was my best friend. All that money she gave me— never once did she ask me to pay it back."

"I wouldn't worry too much," I said. "You bought her a mink coat and God knows what else."

"I bought her—!"

I got up on my feet and scanned the quiet lake. The sun gleamed blindingly on the aluminum boat putting out from Green Acres.

"Maybe you'd like to go freshen up," I said. "Put on a clean blouse."

"What for? You mean we're actually going now?"

"Pretty soon."

Her shadow receded from the wall and fell apart in the rusted mesh of the screen. The rough siding of the cottage wall was warm to my hand. Her shadow had had no cooling effect. There was a uniform warmth all the way to the bottom step, where I pushed off on my own to walk down through the grove. I leaned against one of the trees, resting, and watched the bright shell skim the surface and the herringbone wake spreading and settling beyond. I walked on down to the dock.

I watched his brown back bend to the oars in that sturdy, measured rhythm: the long, clean thrust of the boat at each stroke. It was too bad, in a way, to have won a twenty-year struggle for self-mastery, only to have an obscure P. I from Chicago, of all places, turn up with the loose end of a long string.

I saw him pause with lifted oars and glance over his shoulder. I waved casually and he nodded. He bent again, his course altered to head him into the dock. I closed my eyes against the dazzling reflection and didn't open them again till I heard the light thump of his boat against the piling.

* * * *

He greeted me with the same calm geniality he had shown the morning before.

It's not possible, I thought. No man can isolate himself so completely from current events by will alone. Somebody must have told him something.

But the blue eyes looked at me without rancor, wrinkling at the corners, and he smiled.

"It's you," he said. "Good morning."

They surely would have told him about Pete, I thought. Or maybe, for him, death is simply a transition from one plane of existence to another, and if he grieves, it's in some other way.

"I have someone for you," I said.

He looked puzzled momentarily, then nodded.

"Of course," he said. "But if it involves admission to Green Acres, there is Mr. Prince—"

"It involves a return to Green Acres, and I doubt that Mr. Prince would be useful."

"I'm afraid I don't understand."

"I'll explain, if you have a few minutes."

"Of course."

I squatted on the dock and found a shadowed place on the water that I could look at without pain.

"Twenty-two years ago," I said, "before you were an institution, you were simply a wealthy man, living with your wife and servants on an estate just across the way. One of the servants, a maid, was a woman named Anita McLeod. She was a hard-working girl, pretty, probably, but not overly bright. Being subordinate by nature as well as position, she was easily seduced. She was also strong and healthy, and, in due course, she gave birth to a baby girl."

The boat had drifted from the dock and he dipped an oar tentatively, then changed his mind and went with the drift. An overhanging willow shaded him. It made me envious. Where I was, on the old boards of the dock, the sun was direct. I could feel sweat running down my sides and my hatband was soaked.

"I don't know how Mrs. Lloyd reacted to this or how much she knew about it. My guess is, she knew very little, because the baby was delivered, not by a doctor, but by a midwife named Kate Royal. Mrs. Lloyd would have been aware of the pregnancy and the existence of the baby, but she needn't have known much else unless Anita told her, which Anita probably didn't. Anita was incredibly close-mouthed. She stayed on for a while at Green Acres, then went away. I was told by one source that 'they got sore at her.' But that's only another way of saying she was afraid. Possibly she left on Mrs. Lloyd's death merely for lack of employment. Anyway, she left Green Acres and apparently never went back—except once for a brief, crucial visit."

He was very still in the boat, his healthy brown legs stretched out from the seat, his hands quiet on the oar handles.

"You ought not to be in the sun in your condition," he said.

I straightened and held on for a minute against the fire in my shoulder. I walked along the dock and into the grass nearer the boat. It felt very good in the shade. It would have been a nice place in which to relax and talk over old times.

"I don't know when it happened," I said, "but I know she went back and I don't have to strain for a convincing reason. Anita McLeod had fallen on hard times. With no other place to turn, she came to Green Acres in her vague, not very bright way, claiming paternal support. In her absence, changes had taken place. Calvin Lloyd had experienced a drastic conversion from his previous life of indolence and devoted his days to the rigorous contemplation of inner truth and self-improvement. Green Acres had already become a semi-public trust under the competent direction of Mr. Ward Prince."

I took off my hat and wiped my forehead and the hatband. My breath was a little short. I wished it could be done without so much talk.

"You were two deeply committed, dedicated men. You were many years younger than you are now, and Anita McLeod hit you pretty hard. If the same thing should happen today—but the trouble with things is that they happen in their own time. Anyway, Anita got her settlement—a handsome one, so handsome she couldn't possibly have turned it down. It must have exceeded her wildest hopes. A paid-up annuity, twenty years—"

"It seemed fair," he said abruptly.

The three sudden, unexpected words of acknowledgment were like a cool hand on my brow. I settled into the grass and breathed more easily. He had come a long way over and it couldn't have been an easy passage.

"More than fair," I said. "And I'm sure you were kind to her and told her she could always come to you with any problem and that in your own mind there were no strings attached to the settlement—"

"There were none," he said firmly. "We were prepared at any time to acknowledge the child."

"I'm sure you were. But you had already relinquished the active direction of your institution and the details of executing the agreement were left in other hands."

His eyes narrowed, squinted at me in the filtered shade of the willows.

"Ward Prince," I said, "was a good and loyal servant. But at this point he made the biggest, possibly the only mistake of his career."

"If you're going to tell me that Ward Prince exacted any kind of promise from Anita—"

"I am, and I understand what it must mean to you. With the best of intentions, for the good of the Lloyd Foundation, a wholly philanthropic institution, Mr. Prince tried to put a tight lid on a very small garbage can. In return for the generous settlement, Anita McLeod agreed to waive for all time all claims on the girl's own father and to renounce permanently any recourse to Green Acres, its director, staff or personnel. She also agreed never to reveal the identity of the girl's father to anyone, including the girl herself."

"It would be impossible!" he said. "Such an agreement—"

"As a legal agreement, worthless. No attorney would have accepted it, no court would permit it. But Prince wasn't negotiating with an attorney. He was negotiating with Anita McLeod, a simple, desperate woman, who was about to receive a sum of money that by her standards would make her rich. It wasn't much of a gamble and he insured it; first, by removing Marianne McLeod's birth certificate from the public records, using a man named Sam Galloway, a county employee; and second, by a modest pay-off to Kate Royal, the midwife. He covered the thing admirably, and he might have made it stick, except that Anita McLeod fell in with an evil companion, a Constance Waters, later Traven."

A school of minnows had clustered in the shade just below the surface. I watched them converge on a luckless mosquito, the ripples sudden and shimmering as one of them broke to snag it.

"The Traven woman is almost the start of a new story and we don't have to go into it. Let's just say, Ward couldn't shake her off his back with the same old efficiency. The thing had become more complex than in the old days. You had become more of a symbol than a person. He'd lost touch with you as a man and he would do anything to preserve that symbol. Other factors had crept in. And then people started dying. Finally I came along, with Marianne."

His oars were flopping idly and he sat with his brown hands between his knees, staring at the floor of the boat.

"At first," I said, "I thought it might have been Prince who fathered Marianne. But she was born more than a year before he came to Green

Acres for the first time. Then I got to digging around and found the elaborate pattern of the deception and there was only one person for whom so much thought and worry and painstaking misdirection could possibly be justified."

His head lifted slowly and our eyes met. His were no longer genial or amused. They were simply calm and wide open with acceptance. He was a better man than Prince.

"This seemed like the ideal way," I said. "You just row her across the lake, getting acquainted on the way. I was under pressure to deliver her to the front door, with due process, as a parolee from the Women's State Farm. It was a shoplifting charge and she took a stiff jolt. You'll be able to straighten it out. At least she can be a parolee with a name."

His lips moved soundlessly.

"It won't be easy," I said, because he deserved some preparation. "She lives in a hard little shell. Her defense is a strong offense. She is uncouth and ignorant. She is also capable of warmth and co-operation. She's not anything like Karen, Mr. Lloyd, but then, she didn't have any of Karen's advantages."

I got on my feet and brushed off the seat of my pants.

"I'll get her now," I said. "She's in the cottage."

"Yes," he said. "Please."

When I turned, looking up through the grove, she was standing on the porch, gazing down through the screen.

* * * *

She had changed her sweater for a blouse. Her eyes, over-bright, searched my face.

"Well," she said, "can we go now?"

"Yup," I said.

"Who was that guy in the boat?"

"Mr. Lloyd," I said. "He'll take you home."

"In a boat?"

"It's nice on the lake today."

She looked down at it with suspicion. I walked into the living room and there was a newspaper bundle on a chair. I opened my valise and she had taken none of the things I'd bought her except the blouse. I took my own things out and put the newspaper-wrapped package in with the rest of hers. She came to the kitchen door and watched me.

"I don't get it," she said. "You mean *the* Mr. Lloyd? The owner of the whole thing?"

I had meant to leave it to him, but it occurred to me that she might not believe it from him.

"Mr. Lloyd is your father," I said.

"You're crazy. My father's dead."

"Your mother promised never to tell anyone, even you. It happened when she was working at Green Acres."

Her funny little face worked on it.

"You mean my mother wasn't my father's wife?"

"No."

"They were playing around, huh?"

"Well—he made love to her."

She laughed harshly, then choked it off.

"Then what I am," she said, "I'm really just a bastard."

"It wasn't your fault and nobody cares now."

I picked up the bag and we went out on the porch.

"Boy," she said, "I better watch my step."

"Why?"

"Because if I go over there to live, my father—Mr. Lloyd—he won't like it much. He might pretend, but he won't really. On account of what he did, you know?"

How does she know that? I thought. How does she know? "Your father is a very kind man," I said. "He wants you to live where you belong. All these years he sent money to your mother for you. She saved a lot of it."

"Where is it?" she said."

"It's gone. Connie Traven stole it."

"Connie—no!"

"Yes."

She gave me the hard look and she was fighting the idea, but she would go along finally. All her life she had been led by the nose. She would go on that way for a while, long enough anyway to give it a try with Calvin Lloyd.

I opened the door and we went down the steps and down through the grove to the dock. Lloyd sat quietly in the boat, waiting.

"Hello, Marianne," he said. "It's been a long time."

She looked him over; her right foot was on its outside edge.

"Hi," she said.

He smiled. I don't know what it cost him.

"How about a boat ride?" he asked.

She looked doubtfully at the boat and at me.

"It's time to go," I said. "You'll live in a fine house, have new clothes—"

I handed the valise down and he stowed it between his bare feet.

"Some of her things," I said. "She'll need more."

His smile broadened.

"What girl doesn't?" he said.

"You my father?" Marianne said suddenly.

"Yes," he said, "and glad to be."

He held out his hand and I reached to help her into the boat, but she pulled back.

"Mac—do I have to—?"

"Go ahead," I said. "Ten minutes, you'll be home. Tomorrow you won't know you've ever been anywhere else."

"Will you come and see me?"

"Sure."

"When?"

"Pretty soon. A few days. Go ahead, honey."

She gave him one more long look and we got her into the boat. She sat on the stern seat, very stiff, holding onto both sides.

"Take care of her," I said. "Teach her to eat something besides hot dogs."

Lloyd laughed quietly. I gave the boat a light push and he headed onto the lake. She sat very still, holding on tight. Two strokes carried them thirty feet out and Marianne looked back. I waved and pretty soon she lifted one hand and wiggled her fingers at me, then grabbed the side again quickly. But she remained, twisted on the little seat, looking back.

I stood watching until I couldn't be sure any more whether she was looking back or not. Then I left the dock and started up the slope. Karen Bowman in slacks and sweater came out from behind a tree and stopped in front of me. Her eyes were like purple grapes in her pale face. Her low voice had the sound of meat gristle going through the grinder.

"You son-of-a-bitch," she said.

CHAPTER THIRTY

My face twisted with the reaming pain in my shoulder. I put my hand on the butt of the gun in my pocket and it was clammy.

"Good morning to you too," I said. "Shall we rest in the shade of the trees?"

We walked into the grove and I leaned against a tree, watching her. There was a tiny crevice at one corner of her mouth. It twitched from time to time.

"You fascinate me," she said, "the way a hyena does. But there's no zoo for your breed, is there?"

"I guess not."

"You'll use anybody, even a man like Calvin Lloyd."

I nodded toward the cottage and we went on up there and inside. I sat down on the rumpled couch.

"Your father is quite a great man," I said. "Marianne doesn't amount to much in your world, and Traven was just another guy. But when they get around to dying, they're all the same. Nobody is worth somebody else's life. Nobody."

"Maybe you have more in common with my father than I realized. You're both fanatics."

I was having that rising and falling sensation. She seemed to have two heads, one of them floating in space.

"Well, it's all over now," I said. "It doesn't matter too much. Your friend made a full confession."

"What?"

I managed to find her and get her two heads into one. If I concentrated on it, I could keep them that way. It cut her down to one pair of eyes and one was plenty.

"Your old friend, Ward Prince. He told me the whole thing—how he killed Connie Traven and how he put Nicky on Traven's tail and then on Roberts' and how Pete shot himself in Ward's presence."

There was quite a long silence. Then she said, "Ward Prince? I can hardly believe it. Do the police know? I can't get it through my head—"

"He was pretty convincing."

She had been sitting down, as I remembered. Now she was standing up, staring at me. I let her two heads float slowly apart, then blend again. She came toward me and I ducked. But she hadn't meant any harm. Her hand was on my shoulder lightly.

"I didn't know you were hurt so badly," she said. "I'm sorry. Don't you want to lie down?"

I did and then again I didn't. But I did. Karen stood over the couch, leaning a little as if her breasts were too heavy for her. It wasn't the case. Actually she was a very erect person.

"Are you going to let Ward take the whole rap?" I said. "All by himself?"

"What does that mean, Mac?"

"Well, he wasn't quite convincing enough. His hands were too clean. He was being gallant. I guess he thought you had it coming, his having found a new love and all—"

"Take it easy," she said quietly. "After you rest, we'll go home and get a doctor."

She was doing something, but I couldn't quite make it out and it didn't hurt any. She moved away and I fell off the edge of something. While I was falling I had a dream. I dreamed she had taken my gun away from me and I woke up suddenly and it was true. She was standing in the middle of the room, looking at it.

"I didn't want you to hurt yourself, rolling on it," she said.

"That's thoughtful of you. Maybe you'd like to put it on the mantel, where it won't go off."

She didn't want to. She stood there with it and looked at this and that.

"It won't do any good to shoot me," I said. "That is, it would do some good if you just couldn't stand it to look at me any more."

She was examining the gun. She did it like someone who knew about those things. I began looking for an opportunity to take it away from her, but the chances weren't good. She was too far away. There didn't seem to be much to do but to keep talking.

"Because it was you, wasn't it?" I said. "All the things Ward said he did could have been done by you, just as logically and a lot more believably. Circumstantial evidence is an accumulation of little facts that when you have enough of them, they lead to only one conclusion. That little package of pornography on Pete's bedside table could have been put there by you. And there was only one place it could have come from. There was no reason for you to make such a thing of it, opening it and all, with Pete passed out and you alone with a virtual stranger like me. But you did, and you made sure I looked at it. It was a bold move. It fits you.

"And your car was warm that night when you passed out. It had been on a trip. Your clothes were still on your bed, your girdle still damp with perspiration. And when I got here to the cottage in the morning, there wasn't any car. But Marianne told me he'd had a car the night before, at the place where she worked. The Eldorado.

"You must have known about Marianne, from Ward, since way back when. Pete had a note about her in plain sight on his desk at home. You knew what he was doing and what he would likely find out. Disgrace for your father, a smudge on Green Acres—for a girl with your kind of fix, it could become a horrible prospect."

She was weighing the gun on her palm and her brown eyes mined my face. I don't know how it assayed. I wouldn't have given a nickel for it myself.

"That's the bad part," I said, "the thing about Pete. You could have taken care of Pete some other way. What if he did find out a few things, told you off a little? You could have got over it—"

Her once lovely face was not hers any more.

"Because he thought he would take over!" she yelled. "I could see the respect dribble out of him, and not only for me—for everything Ward and my father had tried to build up all those years!"

"Well," I said, "you set it up pretty good. The thing I don't understand—when did Nicky Royal give you that slap in the face?"

She stood there with the gun and stared at me and suddenly she started to laugh. It was a hard, painful laugh that shuddered through her and got louder and louder. But when I got up on my feet, she tightened with the gun and shut the laugh off.

"Nobody—" she said, gasping—"nobody hit me. I ran into a door. Honest to God, Mac, I ran into a door!"

"Why did it have to be Nicky?" I said. "Did you think you could make him be the one just by mentioning his name?"

"I—don't—know—" I held out my hand.

"Let me have the gun, please, Karen—"

She snatched it out of reach and backed away.

"No! Am I crazy?"

We heard the car then, both of us. There hadn't been any approach. It was just suddenly there and the motor died and it was quiet.

"Police," I told her. "I'm not kidding. Take your chances, Karen. Everybody else has."

"I don't believe you!"

I started for her and she turned, grabbed at the door and got it open. Beyond her, Donovan came down the front walk toward the cottage. She ran to the doorway and stopped. The gun was leveled on Donovan. He took her in and it was a woman and there wasn't anything for him to do but hit the dirt.

As he went down, I yelled at her and she turned, swinging the gun around. It bumped the door jamb and I almost got to her. I was so close that when she squeezed off with the muzzle at her breast I could smell the burning wool of her sweater.

She fell back against me and I tried to ease her down with my good arm. She was very heavy. The best I could do was to hold her for a minute, propped against my legs while she died. She died quietly and without any messiness. It couldn't have been too bad, though a little harder than it had been for Pete.

Donovan held her while I backed off, then let her down on the floor. He was very gentle with her.

* * * *

Afterward we sat on the couch.

"Thanks for coming," I said.

"I had to," he said. "I told 'em I was bringin' you in. It would look funny to show up without you."

"Did you pick up Nick Royal?"

He nodded.

"I hate for it to be a kid like that," he said.

I looked toward where Karen had fallen, but he had covered her with a sheet and I couldn't see any of her any more.

I looked at Donovan again. His suit was stained and wrinkled where he had fallen on it. I wondered how long it would be before I would learn how close behind me he had been.

"Don't look back," he had said.

…Keep moving—don't slow down—don't look back.…

www.ingramcontent.com/pod-product-compliance
Lightning Source LLC
Chambersburg PA
CBHW031129210626
46816CB00015B/1244